D. L. Moody's
Children's
Stories

Children's Stories

D. L. Moody

Christian Focus Publications

DWIGHT LYMAN MOODY
(1837 – 1899)

Dwight L. Moody was born at Northfield, Massachusetts in 1837. After attending school until thirteen, Moody went to work and, at the age of seventeen, moved to Boston to work in a shoe store. Whilst in Boston, he attended a congregational church where, through the influence of his Sunday school teacher, Moody was converted to Christ. Moody later left for Chicago where, as he became a successful a travelling salesman. In 1860 he gave it up to spend his full time in Sunday school and YMCA work.

During the American Civil War, Moody worked among soldiers whilst continuing his involvement with Sunday schools, establishing a Street church and participating in national Sunday school conventions. It was at one of these conventions that he met Ira D. Sankey, who he enlisted as his musical associate.

In 1873, Moody sailed to the British Isles for a two-year tour, which was destined to make him a national figure. They visited York,, Glasgow, Edinburgh and London for a four-month stay where attendance at their meetings reached more that 2.5 million.

Moody preached to millions in his lifetime but always had a deep interest and loving concern in bringing the gospel to children.

This book was presented to

....

on

....

from

....

Train a child in the way he should go.
Proverbs 22:6

ISBN: 1-85792-640-4

© Copyright 2000
Christian Focus Publications Ltd.
Geanies House, Fearn, Ross-shire,
IV20 1TW, Scotland, Great Britain.

Cover design by Catherine Mackenzie

Pinted and bound by Cox and Wyman, Reading

Contents

A little quote

The prodigal son got down very low, but he did not get down low enough to beg; he went to work.

The Lost Kiss

A few years ago, my little girl sometimes got up feeling cross in the mornings. You know how it is when any member of the family does not get up in a good temper; it disturbs the rest of the family. Well, one morning she got up and spoke in a cross way, and I said, "Emma, if you speak in that way again, I shall have to punish you."

Now it was not because I didn't love her, it was for her own good.

Well, that went off all right, but one morning she woke up in a bad mood again. I said nothing, but when she was getting ready to go to school she came up to me and said, "Papa, kiss me."

I said, "Emma, I cannot kiss you this morning."

She said, "Why, Father?"

"Because you have been cross again this morning. I cannot kiss you."

"Why, Papa you've never refused to kiss me before."

"Well, you have been naughty this morning."

"Why don't you kiss me?" she said again.

"Because you've been naughty. You will have to go to school without your kiss."

She went into the other room where her mother was and said, "Mamma, Papa doesn't love me. He won't kiss me. I wish you would go and get him to kiss me."

But her mother said, "You know, Emma, that your father loves you, but you have been naughty."

So she couldn't be kissed, and she went downstairs crying as if her heart would break.

I could not keep down my own tears, and I think I loved her more at that moment than I ever had. When I heard the door close I went to the window and saw her going down the street weeping. I didn't feel good all day. I believe I felt a good deal worse than Emma did, and I was anxious for her to come home.

How long that day seemed, and when she came home at night and asked me to forgive her, how gladly I kissed her, and how happy she went upstairs to her bed.

It is just the same with God. He loves you, and when He chastises you it is for your own good. If you will only come to Him and tell Him how sorry you are, how gladly He will receive you. How happy you will make Him, and oh, how happy you will be yourself.

A Child Legend

There is a beautiful legend about a little girl who was the first-born of a family in Egypt when the destroying angel swept through that land. Consequently, she knew that she might be a victim of the angel of death that night. She asked her father if the blood was sprinkled on the door-posts and he said that he had ordered it to be done. She asked him if he had seen it there and he said no, but he had no doubt that it had been done. He had seen the lamb killed, and had told the servant to attend to it.

The little girl was not satisfied, and urged her father to carry her to the door to see. They found that the servant had neglected to put the blood upon the posts. The child had been exposed to death until they found the blood and sprinkled it on the posts.

See to it that you are safe in Christ.

A Boy's Victory

I remember when holding a meeting in Kansas, I saw a little boy who came up to the window crying. I went to him and said: "My little boy what is your trouble?"

"Why Mr. Moody, my mother's dead, my father drinks, and they don't love me, and the Lord won't have anything to do with me because I am the son of a drunkard."

"You have a wrong idea, my boy," I replied. "Jesus will love you and save you and your father too," and I told him a story of a little boy in an Eastern city.

I told the little boy who was crying about another little boy whose father would never allow hypocritical Christians to come into his house, and would never allow his child to go to Sunday School. But a kind-hearted man got his little boy and brought him to Christ.

One day, when the boy's father had been drinking, he came home and heard his son praying. He went to him and said: "I don't want you to pray any more. You've been along with some of those Christians. If I catch you again I'll flog you."

The boy was filled with God and he couldn't help praying. The door of communication was opened between him and Christ, and his father caught him.

"Didn't I tell you never to pray again?" he said. "If I catch you once more you must leave my house."

Not very long after this when the father had been drinking more than usual, he came in and found the boy offering a prayer.

"Leave this house," he raged, pushing the boy. "Pack up and go."

The little fellow hadn't many things to get together, and he went up to his mother's room.

"Goodbye, mother."

"Where are you going?"

"I don't know where I'll go, but father says I cannot stay here any longer; I've been praying again," he said.

His mother knew it wouldn't help to try and keep the boy when her husband had ordered him away, so she drew him to her and kissed him and said good-bye. Then he went to his brothers and sisters and kissed them good-bye. When he came to the door his father was there and the little fellow reached out his hand — "Goodbye father. As long as I live I will pray for you," and he left the house.

The boy hadn't been gone many minutes when his father rushed after him.

"Son, if that is religion, if it can drive you away from father and mother and home, I want it."

Just as I told this story to the little boy who was crying perhaps I am telling it again to some other child who has a drinking father and mother. Lift your voice, and the news will be carried up to heaven.

A Boy's Story

Some years ago as I was about to close a prayer meeting, a young man got up and urged all those men who had not yet accepted Christ to do so that night. And in closing his speech, he told a story.

"I once had a father and mother who cared more for my soul than for anything else. My father died and my mother was more anxious for me than ever. Sometimes, she would come and put her loving arms around my neck, and she would plead with me to accept Christ. After my father was dead she used to tell me that she was lonely because I wasn't a Christian. I sympathized with her; but declared that I wanted to see a little of the world. I did not want to become a Christian in early life.

Sometimes I would wake up after midnight and hear a voice in my mother's chamber. I would hear my mother crying to God for me, her only child - I was very dear to her. At last, I felt I must either become a Christian or go away from her influence, and so I ran away.

After I had been gone a long time I heard from home indirectly. My mother was sick, and I knew what it meant. She was pining for me, and I knew that her heart was broken on account of me and my wayward life. I thought I would go home and ask my mother to forgive me, but my second thought was that if I did I could not stay under the same roof without becoming a Christian. My rebellious heart said: "I will not go."

When I heard again, my mother was much worse and I thought, suppose my mother should die and I should never see her again - I could never forgive myself. I started for home. There was no train to my native village so I took the coach and arrived just after dark.

The moon was shining as I began the mile-and-a-half walk to my mother's house. On my way, I thought, I would go past the graveyard, climb over the fence and go to the grave where my father was buried.

As I approached, my heart began to beat more quickly, for by the light of the moon I saw a newly-made grave. The whole story was told. My mother had died too, and for the first time in my life this question came stealing over me: who was going to pray for my lost soul now? Father and mother were both gone now. And, young men, I would have given the world if I could have called my mother back, put her arms around my neck and heard her breathe my name in prayer. But her voice was silent for ever. She was gone.

I knelt beside the grave, crying that God might have mercy on me and forgive me. I did not leave until the morning dawned, and by then I believed that God, for Christ's sake, had forgiven my sins, and that my mother's God had become mine.

But, young men, I will never forgive myself. I trampled my mother's prayers and entreaties under my feet. I broke her heart and sent her to her grave. Young men, if you have a godly mother, treat her kindly."

A little quote

I've lived nearly forty years, and
I've learned one thing
if I've learned nothing else;
that no man or woman who treats
his or her father or mother
disrespectfully ever prospers.

Over the River

There was once a minister whose child had just died. Instead of preaching one morning he asked another minister to preach for him. The other minister came and told a story about his home town which had a large river flowing down the middle of it. The minister told how he lived on one side and his daughter on the other. "To tell the truth," he said, "I was never very interested in the people who lived on the other side of the river, until my daughter married and went over there to live. Now every morning I look across that river, and feel very concerned about all the people there.

"Now," said the visiting minister, "Your minister here has lost his child. I think that as this child has crossed a river, the river of death, heaven, the place on the other side of the river, will be dearer to your minister than it ever has been before. His child is now there."

We should also long for heaven. We should look to the other side of this river. Shall we not just let our hearts and affections be set on the other side of the river? We shall soon be in the other world.

Moody and the Children

During the first two or three years that I
attempted to talk in meetings I saw that the
older people did not like it. I had sense
enough to know that I was a bore to them.
Well, I went out onto the street and led
eighteen children into the Sunday School. I
was encouraged - I found that I had
something to do and I kept at that work.
And if I am worth anything to the Christian
Church today, it is as much due to that work
as anything else.

I could not explain Scripture passages to
the children for I did not understand them
at that time, but I could tell stories. I told
them that Christ loved them and died for
them. I did the best I could with what I had,
and God kept giving me more talents.

Let me say, find some work. See if you
can get a Sunday School to teach, and if you
cannot, find other opportunities. When you
have won one soul to Christ, you will want
to win two, and when you get into the
luxury of winning souls it will be a new
world to you, and you will not think of
going back to the world at all.

A Child's Request for Prayer

One day a little child brought me a note. I put it in my pocket and read it when I got home. It was this: "Won't you pray that my mother may come home?"

On inquiry, I found that the child was homeless. Her father was dead and her mother had deserted her and had gone to San Francisco. I must confess it staggered me that she was praying for her mother to come back.

But then some time afterwards another note was handed to me: "You will remember the little child who asked us to pray for her mother to return home. This mother has returned, and was at the meeting with her little child on Friday night." The child now wants us to pray that her dear mother may be converted."

The Little Bell Boy

A mother lay dying. She had been married a second time, and had a son whom her second husband did not like.

This mother sent for me and she said, "Now I am dying from consumption. I have been sick a long time, and since I have been lying here I have neglected my son. He has got into bad company, and he is very, very unkind and he has started swearing. Mr. Moody, I want you to promise me that when I am gone and he has no one to take care of him, that you will look after him."

I promised that I would, and soon after that the mother died. Now, all he had was a stepfather who did not care for him. No sooner was the lady buried than her son ran away and could not be found. The next Sunday I spoke to the children in my Sunday School and I asked them to look for him and if they found him to let me know.

For some time I heard nothing, but one day one of my scholars told me that the boy was a bell boy in a certain hotel. I found him there and spoke to him kindly about Christ, of his love for him, and of what He had done for him. The tears trickled down his cheeks.

I asked the boy if he wanted to know Christ, and he told me he did.

A little boy was with me that night, and he got down upon his knees and prayed with the bell boy. I remember it well, for it was the night before the fourth of July and they were firing off cannon and sky-rockets into the midnight sky. The bell boy climbed up onto the flat roof of the hotel and called upon God for light, aid and comfort.

Today, that boy is an active Christian young man and superintendent of a Sunday School. He is now leading others to Christ.

There is a work for you. Take these children by the hand and lead them to the cross of Christ. They can be gathered into our churches, and be a blessing to the Church of God.

Reaping the Whirlwind

I remember a prominent citizen who told of a sad case which happened in the city of Newcastle-upon-Tyne in the north of England. It was about a very young boy, an only child whose father and mother thought everything of him and did all they could for him. He fell into bad ways, took up with evil characters, and finally joined a gang of thieves.

The boy didn't tell his parents about his behaviour and one day, when he went with the gang, he broke into his parents house. The thieves stayed outside the building, while he crept in and started to steal. He was caught in the act, taken into court, tried, convicted, and sent to the prison for ten years. He worked on and on in the convict's cell, till at last his term was out, and at once he started for home.

When he came back to the town, the young man started down the street where his father and mother used to live. He went to the house and rapped on the door. A stranger opened it and stared him in the face. "No, there's no such person lives here, and where your parents are I don't know," was the only welcome he received. So he turned through the gate and went down the street asking even the children that he met about his folks, but everybody looked blank.

Ten years had rolled by and though that seemed perhaps a short time, how many changes had taken place! Where he had been born and brought up he was now an alien, and unknown even in the old haunts.

At last he found a couple of townsmen who remembered his father and mother. They told him that the old house had been deserted long years ago, that he had been gone but a few months before his father was confined to his house and very soon after, had died broken-hearted. His mother had gone out of her mind.

The young man went to the asylum where his mother was, and went up to her. "Mother, Mother," he cried, "don't you know me? I am your son." But she raved and slapped him on the face and shrieked, "You are not my son," and tore her hair.

He left the asylum more dead than alive, so completely broken-hearted that he died in a few months. Yes, the fruit was long growing, but at the last it ripened to the harvest like a whirlwind.

A little quote

The most devoted love on earth
is the love of a mother
for her child;
but what is it in comparison
to God's love?
Mothers "may forget, yet I will
not forget you," says the Lord.

The Speaking Card

A friend of mine in Philadelphia was going past a drinking saloon one night, when he saw a professing Christian inside who was playing cards. He took a pencil, wrote on a card, and seeing a little boy, said: "My boy, here is some money. I want you to do an errand for me. You see that man at the table where those three are playing cards?"

"Yes I do."

"Well," said my friend, "just take that card to him."

My friend watched the boy as he handed the card to the card player. On the card was written, "You are my witnesses."

The man looked at it, sprang to his feet, and rushing out into the street asked the boy where the card had come from. The boy said, "A man over there gave it to me."

But by that time my friend had slipped away. Remember the lesson of this story "You are my witnesses." Our behaviour should show Christ wherever we are.

Moody's Mother and
Her Prodigal Son

Before I was fourteen years old the first thing I remember was the death of my father. He had been failed in business, and soon after his death the creditors came in and took everything. My mother was left with a large family of children.

One calamity after another swept over the entire household. Twins were added to the family, and my mother fell ill. The oldest son, my brother, was fifteen years old. My mother turned to him for strength in her calamity. But my brother believed that he must leave home to make a fortune. Away he went and became a wanderer.

My mother used to look eagerly for news of her son. She used to send us to the post-office to see if there was a letter from him. We used to come back with the sad news, "no letter." In the evenings we sat beside her and talked about our father; but the moment the name of my brother was mentioned she would hush us into silence.

Some nights when the wind was very high, and the house, which was upon a hill, would tremble at every gust, my mother for my brother who had treated her so unkindly. I used to think she loved him more than all the rest of us put together, and I believe she did. On Thanksgiving day she used to set a chair for him, thinking he would return home.

My family grew up and we boys left home. I sent letters all over the country, but found no trace of my brother. However, one day, while in Boston, news reached me that he had returned.

That day, while my mother was sitting at the door, a stranger was seen coming towards the house, and when he came to the door he stopped. My mother didn't know her son. He stood there with folded arms and a great beard flowing down his chest, and tears trickled down his face.

When my mother saw those tears she cried, "Oh, it is my lost son," and entreated him to come in. But he stood still.

"No, mother," he said, "I will not come in till I hear first that you have forgiven me."

Do you think she was likely to keep him standing there for long? She rushed to the threshold, threw her arms around him, and breathed forgiveness. God will forgive you.

The Saloon-Keeper and His Children

When I first began to work for the Lord there was a businessman who was converted and who stayed in Boston for three months. When it was time for him to leave, the man said to me that there was a fellow living on such a street in whom he was very much interested, and whose boy was in the High School. The boy had said that he had two brothers and a little sister who didn't go to Sunday School because their parents would not let them. This gentleman said: "I wish you would go round and see them."

Well, I went and I found that the parents lived in a drinking saloon. The father was behind the bar and so I stepped up and told him what I wanted. He said he would rather have his sons become drunkards and his daughter a wicked woman, than have them go to our schools.

I thought that it looked pretty dark and that he was fairly bitter towards me, but I went a second time thinking that I might catch him in a better humour. He ordered me out again but I went a third time and found him in a better mood. He said: "You are talking too much about the Bible. Well, I will tell you what I will do. If you teach them something reasonable, like 'Paine's Age of Reason,' they may go."

I talked further to him and finally he said, "If you will read Paine's book, I will read the New Testament."

Well, to get hold of him, I promised, and he got the best of the bargain. We exchanged books and that gave me a chance to call again and talk with his family.

One day the saloon keeper said: "Young man, you have talked so much about church, now you can have a church down here."

"What do you mean?"

"Why, I will invite some friends, and you can come down here and preach to them; not that I believe a word you say, but I do it to see if it will do us chaps any good."

"Very well," I said; "now let us have it distinctly understood that we are to have a certain definite time."

He told me to come at 11 o'clock, saying, "I want you to understand that you are not to do all the preaching."

"How is that?"

"I shall want to talk, and so will my friends."

I said, "Supposing we have it understood that you are to have forty minutes and I fifteen: is that fair?"

Well, he thought it was fair - he was to have the first forty and I the last fifteen minutes.

I went to the saloon, and took a little boy with me, thinking that he might aid me, but the saloon-keeper wasn't there. I thought perhaps he had backed out, but I then learned that his saloon was too small to hold all his friends, and he had gone to a neighbour's. We went there and found two rooms filled.

There were atheists and scoffers there, and the moment I got in they plied me with all sorts of questions. I said I hadn't come to hold any discussion; that they had been discussing for years and had reached no conclusion.

They took up forty-five minutes of time talking, and there were no two who could agree. Then came my turn. I said: "We always open our meetings with prayer; let us pray."

I prayed and thought perhaps someone else would pray before I got through. After I finished, the little boy prayed. I wish you could have heard him. He prayed to God to have mercy upon those men who were talking so against His beloved Son. His voice sounded more like an angel's than a human voice.

After we got up, I was going to speak, but there was not a dry eye in the assembly. One after another went out, and the old man I had been after for months came to me. Placing his hands on my shoulder, and with tears streaming down his face, he said: "Mr. Moody, my children can go to your Sunday School."

They came the next Sunday, and after a few months the oldest boy, a promising young man then in the High School, came upon the platform, and with his chin quivering and the tears in his eyes, said: "I wish to ask these people to pray for me; I want to become a Christian."

God heard and answered our prayers for him.

In all my acquaintances, I don't know of a man whom it seemed more hopeless to reach. I believe if we lay ourselves out for the work there is, any man or woman can be reached and saved. I don't care who he or she is, we can go in the name of our Master and persevere until we succeed. It will not be long before Christ blesses us, no matter how hard their heart is. "We shall reap if we faint not."

"<u>Rover.</u>"

I remember when Dr. Arnold, who has gone to God, was delivering a sermon, he used an illustration. The sermon and text have all gone, but the illustration is fresh upon my mind tonight and brings home the truth.

He said: "You have been sometimes out at dinner with a friend, and you have seen the faithful household dog standing watching every mouthful his master takes. All the crumbs that fall on the floor he picks up, and he seems eager for them, but when his master takes a plate of beef and puts it on the floor and says, 'Rover, here's something for you,' he comes up and smells it, looks at his master, and goes away to a corner of the room."

"He was willing to eat the crumbs, but he wouldn't touch the roast beef — thought it was too good for him." That is the way with a good many Christians. They are willing to eat the crumbs, but not willing to take all God wants. Come boldly to the throne of grace and get the help you need; there is plenty for every man, woman and child.

The Prisoner Weeping for his Children

One day a man of about my age came to me and said he wanted to see me alone. I took him on one side and he told me a story that would make almost any man weep.

He was in a good position—a leading businessman of the community, and he had a beautiful wife and children. He was ambitious to get rich fast. He decided to make a forgery. That is he made some false money and pretended that it was real. In order to cover up that act, he committed other guilty acts and then he fled. He was a fugitive from justice, and he said: "I am now in the torments of hell. Here I am, away from my family, and a reward has been offered for me in my city. Should I go back?"

I said, "I don't know. You had better go to God and ask Him about it. I would not like to give you advice."

You could hear him sob all over that church. He said, "I will go to my room and I will come and see you tomorrow at one o'clock."

The next day the man came to me and he said, "I do not belong to myself, I belong to the law. I have got to go and give myself up. I do not care for myself, but it will disgrace my family, but if I don't I am afraid I will lose my soul."

Eventually I got a letter from him. Some people have said that I ought to take it to Charlestown and read it to the convicts in the State Prison. This letter may keep some man from falling into the same trap and bringing sorrow and gloom upon his loved ones. Let me read this letter to you,

JEFFERSON CITY, Mo., April 8, 1877.

Mr. Moody

Dear BROTHER: When I said goodbye to you in Farwell Hall you said: "When it is all over, write to me." I wrote in December, and I thought then that it would soon be over.

(Let me say here that this letter drew a picture that has followed me all these days. He said he went to his home. He wanted to see his wife, but he did not want his children to know he was there as it might get out among the neighbours, and he wanted to give himself up and not be arrested. After his wife put the children to bed, he peeked into their room, but could not speak to them or kiss them. Fathers, wasn't that hard? And you tell me sin is sweet! There is that man who loved his children as you love yours, and he did not dare to speak to them.)

I wrote to you in December, thinking all would soon be over, but the State was not ready to try me, and so I was let out upon bail till April. Yesterday my case was disposed of, and I received sentence for nineteen years."

(Oh, how sad! how bitter sin is. Pray that God may open the eyes of the blind. Christ came for the recovery of sight to the blind. I hope every sinner will get his eyes opened and see that sin is bitter and not sweet. The time is coming when you have got to leave this earth.)

"Now I am in my prison cell, clothed as a convict. It is all over with me. Pray for me that I may be strengthened. Pray for the loved ones at home; my dear parents and brothers and sisters, and my dear wife and children. And I ask that the attorney, who was very kind to me may be prayed for, that he may become a Christian.

If it is not asking too much of anyone can you please write to me care of penitentiary in Jefferson City, Mo.

" I pray that your labours may be blessed, and when you preach, warn men to beware of the temptation of doing evil; warn them to beware of the ambition for wealth. Prayerfully and tearfully yours."

Dr. Booth's Story

Dr. Booth of New York, was telling me about being in an Eastern country some time ago. He saw a shepherd who wanted to get his flock across a stream. He went into the water and called them by name, but they came down to the bank and bleated, too frightened to follow.

At last he got out of the water and took up two little lambs. He put one inside his coat, and another against his chest, and then he started into the water. The old ones looked up to the shepherd instead of down into the water for they wanted to see their little ones. And so the shepherd got them over the water and led them into the green pastures on the other side.

Sometimes God takes a child to heaven and then the father and mother begin to look up and follow. Sometimes God will take a child to heaven so that his or her parents will long to go to heaven also to be with that child. To go to that place where God has prepared mansions for those who love Him.

Peace

My little boy had some trouble with his sister one Saturday and he did not want to forgive her. That night, when he had knelt down by his mother and said his prayers, I went up to him and said, "Willie, did you pray?"

"I said my prayers."

"Yes, but did you pray?"

"I said my prayers."

"I know you said them, but did you pray?" He hung his head. "You are angry with your sister?"

"Well she had no business to do this and that."

"That has nothing to do with it; you have the wrong idea, my boy, if you think that you have prayed tonight."

You see, he was trying to get over it by saying, "I said my prayers tonight." I find that people say their prayers every night, just to ease their conscience.

I said: "Willie, if you don't forgive your sister, you will not sleep tonight. Ask her to forgive you."

He didn't want to do that. He loves the country, and he has been talking a great deal about the time when he can go into the country and play out-doors. So he said: "Oh, yes, I will sleep well enough; I am going to think about being out there in the country!"

That is the way that we are; we try to think of something else to get rid of the thought of these sins, but we cannot.

I said nothing more to him. I went on studying, and his mother came downstairs. But soon he called his mother and said, "Mother, please go up and ask Emma if she will forgive me." Then I afterwards heard him murmuring in bed, and he was saying his prayers. And he said to me, "Papa, you were right, I could not sleep, and I cannot tell you how happy I am now."

Don't think there is any peace until your sins are put away. My dear friends, the gospel of the Lord Jesus Christ is the gospel of peace.

Very Sad News

I know a mother who lives in Indiana. Some years ago her son came to Chicago. He hadn't been in the city long before he was led astray.

A neighbour happened to be in Chicago, and found him drunk one night in the streets. When that neighbour went home he took the father aside, and told him what he had seen.

It was a terrible blow. When the children were in bed the husband said to his wife, "I have bad news from Chicago today."

She dropped her work in an instant and said: "Tell me what it is."

"Our son was seen on the streets of Chicago drunk."

Neither slept that night, but took their burden to Christ. At daylight the mother said: "I don't know how, when or where, but God has given me faith to believe that our son will be saved."

One week after, that boy left Chicago. He couldn't tell why — an unseen power seemed to lead him to his mother's home, and the first thing he said on coming over the threshold was, "Mother, I have come home to ask you to pray for me."

Soon after, he came back to Chicago a bright and shining light.

A little quote

Someone has said that there were thousands of men in that camp who knew that God could use them, but David was the only one who believed that God would use him. Said David, "Now I will go."

Young Moody's Conversion

When I was in Boston I went to Sunday School. One day the teacher came to the shop I worked in, and put his hand on my shoulder and talked to me about Christ and my soul.

I said, "How strange. This man never saw me till a few days ago, and he is weeping over my sins. I never shed a tear about them."

I understand now what it is to weep for men's souls. I don't remember what he said, but I can feel the power of that young man's hand on my shoulder tonight. It was not long before I was brought into the kingdom of God. I travelled far after that but often thought I would like to see that man again. Some years later I was at Boston again, preaching. A fine looking young man came up the aisle and said, "I should like to speak with you, Mr. Moody; I have often heard my father talk about you."

"Who is your father?" I asked.

"Edward Kemble," was the reply.

"My old Sunday School teacher!" I exclaimed

The young man was called Henry and was seventeen years old. I put my hand on his shoulder just where his father had done, and said, "You are as old as I was when your father put his hand on my shoulder. Are you a Christian, Henry?"

"No, sir," he said; and as I talked to him about his soul with my hand on his shoulder, the tears began to trickle down.

"Come," I said, "I will show you how you can be saved," I prayed with him and read Isaiah chapter 53: '"All we like sheep have gone astray. We have turned every one to his own way."' Do you believe that, Henry? Is that true?" I asked

"Yes, sir, I know that's true and that's what troubles me: I like my own way."

"But there is another sentence yet, Henry: 'The Lord has laid on Him the iniquity of us all.' Do you believe that, Henry?"

"No, I do not, sir."

"Why do you believe one part of God's word and not another. Here are two things against you, and you believe them. Here is one in your favour, but you won't believe it. Why abuse God's word in this way?"

"Well, If Idid, I could be saved."

"I know you could," I replied, "and that's exactly what I want you to do. But you take the bitter, and won't have the sweet with it."

So I reminded him and kept reminding him that "God has laid on Christ the iniquity of us all."

The Child

A number of years ago I went out of Chicago to try and preach and went to a little town where a Sunday School convention was being held. I was a perfect stranger in the place, and when I arrived a man stepped up to me and asked me if my name was Moody. I told him it was and he invited me to his house.

When I got there the man said he had to go to the convention, and asked me to excuse his wife as she, not having a servant, had to attend to her household duties. He put me into the parlour, and told me to amuse myself as best I could till he came back.

I sat there, but the room was dark and l could not read, and I got tired. So I thought I would try and get the children and play with them. I listened for some sound of childhood in the house, but could not hear a single evidence of the presence of little ones.

When my friend came back I said: "Haven't you any children?"

"Yes," he replied, "I have one but she's in Heaven, and I am glad she is there, Moody."

"Are you glad that your child's dead?" I inquired.

He went on to tell me how he had worshipped that child; how his whole life had been bound up in her to the neglect of his Saviour. One day he had come home and found her dying. Upon her death he had accused God of being unjust. He saw some of his neighbours with their children around them. Why hadn't he taken some of them away?

After the funeral the man said: "All at once I thought I heard her little voice calling me, but the truth came to my heart that she was gone. Then I thought I heard her feet upon the stairs; but I knew she was lying in the grave. The thought of her loss almost made me mad. I threw myself on my bed and wept bitterly. I fell asleep, and while I slept I had a dream, but it almost seemed to me like a vision.

"I thought I was going over a barren field, and I came to a river so dark and chill-looking that I was going to turn away. All at once I saw on the opposite bank the most beautiful sight I ever looked at. I thought death and sorrow could never enter into that lovely region. Then I began to see beings all so happy looking, and among them I saw my little child. She waved her little angel hand to me and cried, 'Father, Father, come this way.' I thought her voice sounded much sweeter than it did on earth.

"In my dream I went to the water and tried to cross it, but found it deep and the current so rapid that I thought if I entered, it would carry me away from her forever. I tried to find a boatman to take me over, but couldn't, and I walked up and down the river trying to find a crossing, and still she cried: 'Come this way.'

"All at once I heard a voice come rolling down, 'I am the way, the truth and the life; no man comes to the Father but by me.' The voice awoke me from my sleep, and I knew it was my Saviour calling me, and pointing the way for me to reach my darling child. I am now superintendent of a Sunday-School: I have made many converts; my wife has been converted, and we will, through Jesus as the way, see our child one day."

The Child and President Lincoln

During the war, a young man, on the front line was sentenced to be shot. He had enlisted, though not obliged to. He had gone with another young man. They were what we would call "mates."

One night, this companion was ordered out on picket duty, and he asked the young man to go for him. The next night he was ordered out himself; and having been awake two nights, and not being used to it, he fell asleep at his post. He was discovered, and was tried and sentenced to death. The President had ordered that no interference would be allowed in cases of this kind. This sort of thing had become too frequent, and it must be stopped.

When the news reached the father and mother in Vermont it nearly broke their hearts. The thought that their son would be shot was too great for them. They had no hope that he would be saved by anything they could do. But they had a little daughter who had read the life of Abraham Lincoln, and who knew how he had loved his own children. She said: "If Abraham Lincoln knew how my father and mother loved my brother he wouldn't let him be shot."

The little girl thought the matter over and made up her mind to see the President. She went to the White House, and the sentinel when he saw her imploring looks, passed her in. When she came to the door and told the private secretary that she wanted to see the President, he could not refuse her either.

She came into the chamber and found Abraham Lincoln surrounded by his generals and counsellors, and when he saw the little country girl, he asked her what she wanted. The little girl told her plain, simple story — how her brother, whom her father and mother loved very dearly, had been sentenced to be shot; how they were mourning for him, and if he was to die in that way it would break their hearts.

The President's heart was touched with compassion, and he immediately sent a dispatch cancelling the sentence and giving the boy a parole so that he could come home and see his father and mother. I just tell you this to show you how Abraham Lincoln's heart was moved by compassion for the sorrow of that father and mother. And if he showed so much, do you think the Son of God will not have compassion upon you if you only take that crushed, bruised heart to him?

Faith

A little girl lived with her parents in a small village. One day the news came that her father had joined the army.Not long after that the landlord demanded the rent. The mother told him that her husband had gone into the army and that she didn't have it.

The landlord was a hard-hearted man, and he stormed and said that they must leave the house; he wasn't going to keep people who couldn't pay the rent.

After he had gone, the mother threw herself into the armchair, and began to weep bitterly. Her little girl, whom she had taught to pray in faith (but it is more difficult to practise than to preach), came up to her, and said, "What makes you cry mamma? I will pray to God to give us a little house, and he will."

What could the mother say? So the little child went into the next room and began to pray. The door was open, and the mother could hear every word.

"Oh God, you have come and taken away father, and mamma has no money, and the landlord will turn us out because we can't pay, and we will have to sit on the doorstep, and mamma will catch cold. Give us a little home." She waited as if for an answer, and then added, "Won't you, please, God?"

The little girl came out of the room quite happy, expecting a house to be given them and the mother felt reproved.

I can tell you however, she has never paid any rent since, for God heard the prayer of that little one, and touched the heart of the cruel landlord. God give us the faith of that little child, that we may likewise expect an answer.

Saved in Weakness

Doctor Andrew Bonar told me how, in the Highlands of Scotland, often a sheep would wander off onto the rocks and get stuck. The grass on these mountains is very sweet and as the sheep like it, they will jump down ten or twelve feet to reach it, and then they can't jump back again.

The sheep may be there for days, but the shepherd, though he hears them bleating in distress, will wait until they have eaten all the grass and are so faint they cannot stand. Only then will he put a rope around him and pull that sheep up out of the jaws of death.

Why don't they go down there when the sheep first gets there? I asked.

"Ah!" he said, "they are so very foolish they would dash right over the precipice and be killed if they did!"

And that is the way with men, they won't go back to God till they have no friends and have lost everything. If you are a wanderer, I come to tell you that the Good Shepherd will bring you back the moment you have given up trying to save yourself and are willing to let Him save you His own way.

Little Moody at School

I remember when I was a boy, I used to go to a certain school in New England, where we had a quick-tempered teacher who used to rule the school by law. He always kept a cane, and it was, "If you don't do this, and don't do that, I'll punish you." I remember many a time this cane being laid upon my back - I can almost feel it now.

After a while, somebody began to get up a movement in favour of controlling the school by love. A great many said, "You can never do that with those unruly boys," but after some talk it was at last decided to try it. I remember how we thought of the good time we would have that winter when the cane would no longer be used. We thought we would then have all the fun we wanted.

I remember who the teacher was — it was a lady — and she opened the school with prayer. We hadn't seen it done before and we were impressed, especially when she prayed that she might have the grace and strength to rule the school with love.

Well, the school went on for several weeks and we saw no cane, but at last the rules were broken, and I think I was the first boy to break them. I was told by the teacher to wait till after school and then she would see me. I thought the cane was coming out, and stretched myself up in warlike attitude.

After school, however, I didn't see the cane. Instead, the teacher sat down by me and told me how she loved me, and how she had prayed to be able to rule that school by love. She concluded by saying, "I want to ask you one favour—that is, if you love me, try and be a good boy."

I never gave her trouble again. She just put me under grace. And that is what the Lord does. God is love, and he wants us all to love Him.

The Drunken Boy Reclaimed

Not long ago a young man went home late. It had become a habit and his father had begun to believe that he had gone astray.

One night, the father told his wife to go to bed and waited for his son to comee home. The boy came home drunk, and his father told him never to enter his house again. He shut the door, then went into the parlour and thought: "I may be to blame for his conduct. I have never prayed with him. I did not warn him of the dangers of the world."

He put on his coat and hat, and went out to find his son eagerly asking a policeman, "Have you seen my boy ?" "No."

On he went till he met another. "Have you seen anything of my son?" He ran from one to another all that night, but not until the morning did he find him.

The man took his son by the arm and led him home, keeping him till he was sober. Then he said, "My dear boy, please forgive me; I never prayed for you, I ledyou astray, and I want your forgiveness."

The boy was touched, and what was the result? Within twenty-four hours he became a convert and gave up drinking alcohol

A little quote

There are three thoughts that I
have tried to bring out: that God is
love; that His love is unchangeable; that His love is everlasting.
The fourth thought is this: that
His love is unfailing.
Your love is not.

The Repentant Son

A bad boy ran away from home. He gave his father a lot of trouble. He refused to come home and be forgiven, and help his father. He even made fun of his parents.

One day, a letter came, telling him that his father was dead. At first he decided he would not go to the funeral, but then he thought it would be a shame not to pay some little respect to the memory of so good a man; and so, he went home.

He sat through the funeral, saw his father buried, and came back with the rest of the friends to the house, his heart as cold and stony as ever. But when the will was read, the ungrateful son found that his father had remembered him along with the rest of the family. He had left him an inheritance with the others, who had not gone astray.

This broke his heart . His father, during all the years in which he had been so wicked had never ceased to love him.

That is just what our Father in Heaven does with us. This is how Jesus cares for those who refuse to give their hearts to Him. He loves them in spite of their sins, and it is this love which, more than anything else, brings hard-hearted sinners to their knees.

Waiting for Jesus

I remember seeing a story in the papers some time ago. A family in a Southern city had gone down with yellow fever. It had been raging there, and very stringent sanitary rules were in operation. The moment anybody died, a cart came around and took the coffin away.

The father was taken sick and died and was buried, and then the mother fell ill with it. The neighbours were afraid of the plague, and did not dare to go into the house.

The mother had a little son and was anxious about her boy. She feared that he would be neglected when she was called away, so she called the little fellow to her bedside. "My boy," she said. "I am going to leave you, but Jesus will come to you when I am gone."

The mother died, the cart came along and she was laid in the grave. The neighbours would have liked to take the boy, but were afraid of the disease, so he wandered about and finally started up to the place where they had laid his mother. There, he sat down on the grave and wept himself to sleep.

Next morning the boy awoke and realized his position - alone and hungry. A stranger came along and seeing the little fellow sitting on the ground, asked him what he was waiting for.

"I am waiting for Jesus," he said, remembering his mother's words, and told the man the whole story.

The man's heart was touched, tears trickled down his cheeks, and he said, "Jesus has sent me," to which the boy replied, "You have been a good while coming, sir."

He was provided for, and so it is with us. To wait for results we must have courage and patience, and God will help us.

Moody in the Far West

I remember when I went to California, just to try and get a few souls saved on the Pacific coast, I went into a school there to teach.

Well, we got out the blackboard, and the lesson was on "Lay up for yourselves treasures in heaven." I asked the class teacher to write the lesson on the board. "Suppose we write on that board some earthly treasures? And we will begin with *gold*."

Everyone understood this for they had all had come to the Pacific coast hoping fo find it.

"Well we will put down *houses* next and then *land*. Next we will put down *fast horses*." They all understood what fast horses were — they knew a good deal more about fast horses than they knew about the kingdom of God.

"Next we will put down *tobacco*." The teacher disagreed. "Put it down," said I, "many a man thinks more of tobacco than he does of God.

"Next put down *rum*." The teacher strongly objected to this. He didn't like to put it down at all.

"Write it down," I said. "Many a man will sell his reputation, his home, his wife, his children, everything he has, for rum. It is the god of some men. Many here are ready to sell their present, and their eternal welfare for it. Put it down," and down it went.

"Now," said I, "suppose we put down some of the heavenly treasures. Put down *Jesus* to head the list, then *heaven*, then *River of Life*, then *Crown of Glory*."

I went on until the column was filled, and then just drew a line and showed the heavenly and the earthly things in contrast. My friends, they could not stand comparison. If a man just does that, he cannot but see the superiority of the heavenly over the earthly treasures.

Well, it turned out that the teacher was not a Christian. He had gone to California on the usual hunt—gold; and when he saw the two columns placed side by side, the excellence of the one over the other was irresistible, and he was the first soul God gave me on the Pacific coast. He accepted Christ, and that man came to the station when I was coming away and blessed me for coming to that place.

Lost in the Deep

I read some time ago of a vessel which had been off on a whaling voyage and had been gone about three years. I saw the account in print somewhere lately, but it happened a long time ago.

The father of one of those sailors had charge of the lighthouse. He was expecting his boy to come home for it was time for the whaling vessel to return.

One night there was a terrible gale, and the father fell asleep. While he slept his light went out, and when he awoke, he looked towards the shore and saw there had been a vessel wrecked. He at once went to see if he could save someone who might be still alive. The first body that came floating towards the shore was, to his great grief, the body of his own son! He had been watching for him for many days, and he had been gone for three years. Now the boy had at last come in sight of home and had perished because his father had let his light go out! I thought, what an illustration of fathers and mothers today who have let their light go out and haven't instructed their children in the word of God, prayed for them or shown them a Christian life and witness.

The Stolen Boy

Many years ago a boy was kidnapped in London. Years passed and his mother prayed but never gave up hope.

One day a boy was next door sweeping a chimney, and by some mistake came down the wrong chimney. When he came down the chimney he found himself in the wrong sitting-room. It was the sitting room of the mother who had lost her little boy all those years ago. Something triggered the little chimney sweep's memory. The room was familiar. Then as he stood there looking, his mother came in. Even though the little boy stood there covered with rags and soot, she recognised him immediately.

Did she wait until he was washed before she took him in her arms? No, indeed; it was her own boy. She immediately took him into her arms and hugged him, crying for joy.

Will God wait for you to do good works, be a better person before he takes you to his heart? Of course not! Believe in the Lord Jesus Christ and you will be saved.

The Happy Home

A little girl came home from church and, sitting on her father's knees, said, "Papa, you have been drinking again."

This troubled him. If his wife had said it, he would have lost his temper and bought more alcohol, but his child acted like an angel. He came to church with her and he found out how he might be saved. And now that home is a little heaven.

Over the Mountains

A mother's child was dying. The child asked her: "What are those clouds and mountains that I see so dark?"

"Eddy," said his mother, "there are no clouds or mountains, you are mistaken."

"But I see great mountains, and dark clouds, and I want you to take me in your arms and carry me over the mountains."

"Ah," said the mother, "pray to Jesus, He will carry you safely. Unbelief is coming upon you, my child. Pray that the Lord will be with you."

The two prayed, but the boy turned to her and said: "Do you hear the angels, mother, calling for me? But I can't go!"

"Darling, pray to Jesus, only he can take you."

The boy closed his eyes and prayed, and when he opened them, he smiled and said, "Jesus has come to carry me over the mountains."

Dear sinner, Jesus is ready and willing to carry you over the mountains of sin, and over your mountains of unbelief. Give yourself to Him.

Emma's New Muff

I remember a time when my little girl was pestering her mother to get her a muff, and so one day her mother brought one home. There was a storm going on outside, but she very naturally wanted to go out and try her new muff.

I went out with my daughter, and I said, "Emma, better let me take your hand," but she wanted to keep her hands in her muff, and so she refused. By and by Emma came to an icy place, her little feet slipped, and down she went. When I helped her up she said, "Papa, give me your little finger."

"No, Emma, just take my hand."

"No, no, Papa, give me your little finger."

Well, I gave my finger to her, and for a little way she got along nicely, but pretty soon we came to another icy place, and again she fell. This time she hurt herself a little, and she said, "Papa, give me your hand," and I gave her my hand, and closed my fingers about her wrist, and held her up so that she could not fall.

Just so, God is our keeper. He is wiser than we are.

Little Jimmy

A friend of mine took his Sunday School out on the streetcars once. A little boy was allowed to sit on the platform of the car, when by some mischance he fell, and the whole train passed over him. They had to go on a half a mile before they could stop.

They went back and found that the poor little fellow had been cut to pieces. Two teachers went back with the remains. Then came the terrible task of telling the parents .

They found the family at dinner. They told the father first. He came out with the napkin in his hand, and my friend said to him "I have very bad news to tell you. Your little Jimmy has been run over by the cars."

The poor man turned deathly pale and rushed into the room crying out, "Dead, dead." The mother sprang to her feet. When she heard the sad story she fainted.

My friend said to me, "I wouldn't tell news like that again if you gave me the whole of Chicago. I never suffered so much. I have a son too. Yet I would rather have a train a mile long run over him than that he should die without God and without hope."

What is the loss of a child compared to the loss of a soul?

Sammy and his Mother

At one time my sister had trouble with her little boy, and his father said, "Sammy, ask your mother's forgiveness."

The little boy said he wouldn't, to which his father replied, "You must. If you don't go and ask your mother's forgiveness, I shall have to put you to bed."

He was a bright, nervous little boy, never still a moment, and his father thought he would be afraid of being put to bed. But he still would not ask for forgiveness, so they put him to bed.

The father went to his business, and when he came home at noon he said to his wife: "Has Sammy asked your forgiveness?"

"No," she said, "he hasn't."

So the father went and asked, "Why don't you ask your mother's forgiveness?"

The boy shook his head, "Won't do it."

"But, Sammy, you have got to."

"Couldn't."

The father went to his office, and stayed all the afternoon. When he came home he asked his wife, "Has Sammy asked your forgiveness?"

"No, I took something up to him and tried to have him eat, but he wouldn't."

So the father went up to see him, and said, "Now, Sammy, just ask your mother's forgiveness, and you may come down to supper with us."

"Couldn't do it."

The father coaxed, but the little fellow "couldn't do it." That was all they could get out of him. You know very well he could, but he didn't want to.

Now, the hardest thing a man has to do is to become a Christian, and it is the easiest. That may seem a contradiction, but it isn't. The hard point is because he doesn't want to. The hardest thing for a man to do is to give up his will.

That night they went to bed and they thought surely early in the morning, he will be ready to ask his mother's forgiveness. The father went to him—that was Friday morning—to see if he was ready to ask his mother's forgiveness, but he "couldn't."

The father and mother felt so bad about it they couldn't eat. Perhaps Sammy thought that his parents didn't love him. Many sinners think the same thing because God won't let them have their own way.

The father went to his business, and when he came home he said to his wife, "Has Sammy asked your forgiveness?"

"No."

So he went to the little fellow and said, "Now, Sammy, are you going to ask your mother's forgiveness?"

"Can't," and that was all they could get out of him. The father couldn't eat any dinner; it was like death in the house. It seemed as if the boy was going to conquer his father and mother. Instead of his little will being broken, it looked very much as if he was going to break theirs.

Late Friday afternoon, "Mother, mother, forgive," says Sammy — "me."

The little fellow said "me," and he sprang to his feet and said: "I have said it, I have said it. Now, take me down to see father." And when he came in he said, "I've said it, I've said it."

Oh, my friends, it is so easy to say, "I will arise and go to my God." It is the most reasonable thing you can do. Isn't it an unreasonable thing to be stubborn and refuse to turn to God?

Come right to God just this very hour. "Believe in the Lord Jesus Christ and you will be saved."

In Jail

I remember a mother who heard that her boy was impressed at one of our meetings. She said her son was a good enough boy, and he didn't need to be converted. I pleaded with that mother, but all my pleading was of no account. I tried my influence with the boy; but when I was pulling one way she was pulling the other, and of course her influence prevailed. Naturally it would.

Well, to make a long story short, some time after, I happened to be in the County Jail and I saw him there.

"How did you get here?" I asked; "Does your mother know where you are?"

"No, don't tell her; I came in under an assumed name, and I am going to jail for four years. Do not let my mother know of this," he pleaded; "she thinks I am in the army."

How awful for that poor mother who was mouring over her boy, thinking he had died on the battlefield or in a Southern hospital.

What a blessing he might have been to that mother, if she had only helped us to bring him to Christ.

The Little Orphan

When I was in Europe, Mr. Spurgeon told me a story of a boy who was in an orphanage. This little boy came up to him and said, "Mr. Spurgeon, would you allow me to speak to you?"

He said, "Certainly, get upon my knee."

The little fellow got up and said, "Mr. Spurgeon, supposing that your mother and father were dead, and that you were put into this institution. And supposing there were other little boys who had no father or mother, but who had cousins and uncles and aunts who brought them fruit and candy and a lot of things. Don't you think that you would feel bad? Cause that's me."

Why, Mr. Spurgeon put his hand in his pocket and gave the little fellow some money right off. The little fellow had pleaded his cause well.

When men come to God and tell their story—I don't care how vile you are, I don't care how far down you have got, I don't care how far off you have wandered— if you will tell it all into His ear, the relief will soon come.

The Praying Child

I once knew a little girl who lay upon her death-bed. She had given herself to God, and was distressed only because she could not work for Him actively among the lost. Her minister visited her, and hearing her complaint, told her that there from her sick-bed she could offer prayers for those whom she wished to see turning to God. He advised her to write the names down, and then to pray earnestly; and then he went away and thought of the subject no more.

Soon a feeling of great religious interest sprang up in the village, and the churches were crowded nightly. The little girl heard of the progress of the revival, and inquired anxiously for the names of the saved.

A few weeks later the little girl died, and among a roll of papers that was found under her little pillow, was one bearing the names of fifty-six persons, every one of whom had been converted in the revival. By each name was a little cross, by which the girl had checked off the names of the converts as they had been reported to her.

Prayer Answered

A few years ago, in the city of Philadelphia, a mother had two sons. They were breaking her heart, and at the prayer-meeting she got up and presented them for prayer.

The boys had been on a drunken spree and she knew that their end would be a bad one. So she went among these Christians and said, "Cry to God for my two boys."

The next morning the boys agreed to meet on the corner of Market and Thirteenth Streets — though they knew nothing about our meeting there. While one was at the corner, waiting for his brother, he followed the people flooding into the meeting. God met him there and that he was convicted of sin and found his way to Christ.

Just a little later, his brother came and found the place too crowded to enter, so he, too, went curiously into another meeting and found Christ, and went home happy.

When the first son got home, he told his mother what the Lord had done. The second son came with the same news. One boy spoke at the young converts' meeting, and afterwards the other got up and said: "I am that brother, and there isn't a happier home in Philadelphia than ours."

The Orphan's Prayer

A child whose father and mother had died, was taken into another family. The first night she asked if she could pray as she used to do, and they said, "Oh, yes."

She knelt down, and prayed as her mother taught her; and when that was ended she added a little prayer of her own: "Oh God, make these people as kind to me as father and mother were." Then she paused and looked up, as if expecting the answer, and added: "Of course He will."

How sweetly simple was that little one's faith; she expected God to "do," and, of course she got her request.

Willie Asks Pardon and Prays

My little boy, has been sick and in the habit of waking up every morning at six o'clock, an hour before I want to wake. One day he woke up at half past five, and his mother told him he must keep still for an hour and a half. He kept making a noise, till at last his mother had to speak sharply to him. When I woke I found him sobbing.

I said, "Willie, what's the matter?"

Well, he was pretty angry with his mother. He got out of bed and knelt down, and I said, "What are you going to do?"

"I'm going to say my prayers."

I told him God wouldn't hear his prayer while he was angry with his mother. If you bring your prayers to God and have anything against your brother you need not pray.

Well, the little fellow went off upstairs, and by and by he went up and asked his mother to forgive him, and then he prayed and went off with a light heart and kept a light heart all day.

Christ says, "You can get victory through Me." With the love of God in us we can speak kindly to those who have angered or annoyed us.

A Singular Story

When I was a youngboy — before I was a Christian — I was in a field one day with a man who was hoeing. He was weeping, and he told me a story, which I never forgot.

When he left home, his mother gave him this text:

"Seek first the kingdom of God."

But he paid no attention to it. He said that when he got settled in life, and his ambition to get money was gratified, it would be time enough then to seek the kingdom of God.

The man went from one village to another and couldn't get work. When Sunday came he went into a village church, and to his great surprise, the minister gave out the text:

"Seek first the kingdom of God."

The text went down to the bottom of the man's heart. He thought that it was his mother's prayer following him, and that someone must have written to that minister about him. He felt very uncomfortable, and when the meeting was over he could not get that sermon out of his mind.

He went away from that town, and at the end of the week, he went into another church and heard the minister give out the same text,

"Seek first the kingdom of God."

He felt sure this time that it was the prayers of his mother, but he said calmly and deliberately, "No, I will get wealthy first."

For a few months the man said that he didn't go into a church, but the first place of worship he went to afterwards, a third minister preached from the same text.

He tried to drown—to stifle his feelings; tried to get the sermon out of his mind, and resolved that he would keep away from church altogether, and for a few years he did keep out of God's house.

"My mother died," he said, "and the text kept coming up in my mind, and I said I will try and become a Christian." The tears rolled down his cheeks as he said, "I could not; no sermon ever touches me; my heart is as hard as that stone," (pointing to one in the field). I couldn't understand what it was all about.

I went to Boston and got converted, and the first thought that came to me was this man. When I got back, I asked my mother, "Is Mr. L— living in such a place?"

"Didn't I write to you about him?" she

asked. "They have taken him to an insane asylum. When ever anybody goes to see him he points with his finger up there and tells him to "seek first the Kingdom of God."

There was that man with his eyes dull with the loss of reason, but the text had sunk into his soul—it had burned down deep.

When I got home again, my mother told me he was in her house, and I went to see him. I found him in a rocking chair, with that vacant, idiotic look upon him. Whenever he saw me he pointed at me and said: "Young man, seek first the kingdom of God." Reason was gone, but the text was there.

Last month when I was laying my brother down in his grave I could not help thinking of that poor man who was lying so near him, and wishing that the prayer of his mother had been heard, and that he had found the kingdom of God.

Mrs. Moody teaching her Child

There was a time when our little boy did
not like to go to church, and would get up
in the morning and say to his mother, "What
day is tomorrow?" "Tuesday."

"Next day?" "Wednesday."

"Next day ?" "Thursday;" and so on, till
he came to the answer, "Sunday."

"Dear me," he said.

I said to the mother, "We cannot have our
boy grow up to hate Sunday in this way;
that will never do. That is the way I used to
feel when I was a boy - I used to look upon
Sunday with a certain amount of dread. Very
few kind words were associated with the
day. I don't know that the minister ever put
his hand on my head. I don't know that the
minister ever noticed me, unless it was
when I was asleep in the gallery, and he
woke me up. This kind of thing won't do.
We must make Sunday the most attractive
day of the week; not a day to be dreaded;
but a day of pleasure."

Well, the mother took the work up with
this boy. Bless those mothers in their work
with the children. Sometimes I feel as if I
would rather be the mother of John Wesley
or Martin Luther or John Knox than have

all the glories in the world. Those mothers who are faithful with the children God has given them will not go unrewarded.

My wife went to work and took those Bible stories and put those blessed truths in a way that the child could understand, and soon the feeling of dread for Sunday with the boy was the other way,"

"What day's tomorrow?" he would ask.

"Sunday."

"I am glad."

And if we make those Bible truths interesting — break them up in some shape so that the children can get at them, then they will begin to enjoy them.

A little quote

After I am dead and gone,
I would rather have a man come to
my grave and drop a tear, and say,
"Here lies the man who converted
me: who brought me to
the cross of Christ"
I would rather have this
than a column of pure gold
built in my honour.
If a man wants to be useful,
follow Christ.

A Bad Boy

A father had a prodigal son, and the boy had sent his mother down to the grave with a broken heart. One evening the boy went out as usual to spend the night in drinking and gambling, and his old father, as he was leaving, said, "My son, I want to ask a favour of you tonight. You have not spent an evening with me since your mother died. Now please stay at home with me?"

"No," said the young man, "it is lonely here, and there is nothing to interest me, and I am going out."

The old man prayed and wept, and at last said,"My boy you are killing me as you have killed your mother. These hairs are growing white, and you are sending me too, to the grave."

Still the boy would not stay, and the old man said: "If you are determined to go to ruin, you must go over this old body tonight. I cannot resist you. You are stronger than I, but if you go out you must go over this body."

And he laid himself down before the door, and that son walked over the form of his father, trampled the love of his father underfoot, and went out.

Two Boys and Two Fathers

There were once two fathers . One lived on the Mississippi River. He was wealthy. Yet, he would have freely given it all, if he could have brought back his son from an early grave. One day that boy was carried home unconscious. They did everything they could to restore him, but in vain.

"He must die," said the doctor.

"But, doctor," said the agonized father, "can you do nothing to bring him to consciousness, even for a moment?"

"That may be," said the doctor; "but he can never live."

Time passed, and after a terrible suspense, the father's wish was gratified. "My son," he whispered, "the doctor tells me you are dying."

"Well," said the boy, "you never prayed for me; will you pray for my lost soul now?"

The father wept. It was true he had never prayed. He was a stranger to God. And in a little while that soul, unprayed for, passed into eternity. Oh, father if your boy was dying, and he called on you to pray, would you pray? Have you learned this sweetest lesson of heaven on earth, to know your God? And before this evil world has taken your dearest treasures will you learn to lead your little ones to a children's Christ?

What a contrast is the other father? He too, had a lovely boy, and one day he came home to find him at the gates of death. "A great change has come over our boy," said the weeping mother: "it seems now as if he were dying fast."

The father went into the room and placed his hand on the forehead of the little boy. He could see the boy was dying. He could feel the cold damp of death.

"My son, do you know you are dying?"

"No; am I?"

"Yes; you are dying?"

"And shall I die today?"

"Yes, my boy, you cannot live till night."

"Well, then, I shall be with Jesus, tonight, won't I, Father?"

"Yes my son, you will spend tonight with the Saviour."

All who read this remember that children learn early. You may have children or you may be a child yourself. But remember that you should instruct your children that their souls are much more valuable and important than any position or success that they may have in life.

The Hand on Moody's Head

I remember when I was a boy, I went several miles from home with an older brother. That seemed to me the longest visit of my life. It seemed that I was then further away from home than I had ever been before, or have ever been since.

While we were walking down the street we saw an old man coming toward us, and my brother said, "There is a man that will give you a cent. He gives every new boy that comes into this town a cent."

That was my first visit to the town, and when the old man came opposite us he looked around, and my brother, not wishing me to lose the cent, and to remind the old man that I had not received it, told him that I was a new boy in the town.

The old man took off my hat, placed his trembling hand on my head, and told me I had a Father in heaven. It was a kind, simple act, but I feel the pressure of the old man's hand upon my head today. You don't know how much you may do by just speaking kindly.

The Smiling Child

A minister once said to me, "Look at the family in the front seat, I will tell you their story. All that family were won by a smile."

"Why," said I, "how's that?"

"Well," said he, "as I was walking down a street one day I saw a child at a window; she smiled, and I smiled, and we bowed. So it was the second time; I bowed and she bowed. Soon there was another child, and I continued to look and bow."

"Soon the group grew, and then one day as I went by, a lady was with them. I didn't know what to do. I didn't want to bow to her, but I knew the children expected it, and so I bowed to them all.

One Sunday, the children followed me when I went to church. And because I had been kind to them, they thought I was the greatest minister, and that their parents must hear me preach.

And to make a long story short, the father and mother and five children were converted, and they are going to join our church next Sunday."

Won to Christ by a smile! We must get the wrinkles out of our brows, and we must have smiling faces.

The Orange Boy

One day as a young lady walked up the street, she saw a little boy running out of a shoemaker's shop, and a shoemaker chasing him. The boy had not run far when the shoemaker threw something at him, and he was struck in the back. The boy stopped and began to cry.

The Spirit of the Lord touched that young lady's heart, and she went to the boy. She asked him if he was hurt and he replied that it was none of her business.

She asked the boy if he went to school and he said, "No."

"Well, why don't you go to school?"

"Don't want to."

She asked him if he would not like to go to Sunday School. "If you will come," she said, "I will tell you beautiful stories and read nice books."

She said that if he would go, she would meet him on the corner of a street which they should agree upon. He at last consented, and the next Sunday, true to his promise, he waited for her at the place designated.

When they met, the lady took the boy by the hand and led him into the Sunday School.

"Can you give me a place to teach this little boy?" she asked of the superintendent.

The man looked him; they didn't have any little ones in the school, but a place was found in a corner, and she tried to win that soul for Christ.

The little boy had never heard anybody sing so sweetly before, and when he went home, he was asked where he had been.

He told his mother he had been to Sunday School, but his father and mother told him he must not go there any more or he would get a flogging.

The next Sunday the boy went, and when he came home he got the promised flogging. He went again and got a flogging, and then again, with the same result. At last he said to his father, "I wish you would flog me before I go, and then I won't have to think of it when I am there." The father said, "If you go again I will kill you."

It was the father's custom to send his son out on the street to sell articles to the passers-by, and he told the boy that he might have the profits of what he sold on Saturday. The little fellow hastened to the young lady's house and said to her, "Father said that he would give me every Saturday to myself, and if you will just teach me, then I will come to your house every Saturday afternoon."

I wonder how many young ladies would give up their Saturday afternoons just to lead one boy into the kingdom of God.

Every Saturday afternoon he was at her house, and she tried to tell him the way to Christ. At last the light of God's spirit broke upon his heart.

One day, while he was selling his wares at the railway station, a train of cars approached unnoticed and passed over both his legs. A doctor was summoned, and as he arrived, the little boy saked, "Doctor, will I live to get home?"

"No," said the doctor, "you are dying."

"Will you tell my mother and father that I died a Christian?"

They took home the boy's body, and with it, the last message that he had died a Christian.

Oh, what a noble work was that young lady's in saving the little wanderer ! How precious the remembrance to her! When she goes to heaven she will not be a stranger there. He will take her by the hand and lead her to the throne of Christ. She did the work cheerfully. Oh, may God teach us what our work is that we may do it for His glory.

Love

In Chicago a few years ago, there was a little boy who went to one of the mission Sunday Schools. His father moved to another part of the city about five miles away, and every Sunday that boy came past thirty or forty Sunday Schools to the one he attended.

One Sunday, a lady who was out collecting scholars for a Sunday School met him and asked why he went so far, past so many schools. "There are plenty of others," said she, "just as good."

He said, "They may be as good, but they are not so good for me."

"Why not?" she asked.

"Because they love a fellow over there," he answered.

Ah, love won him. How easy it is to reach people through love. Sunday School teachers should win the affections of their scholars if they wish to lead them to Christ.

A Little Boy Converts his Mother

I remember once that I was trying to get to know a family I had come in contact with in order to teach them about Christ. However, time and again I failed. Then one night in a meeting I noticed one of the little boys of that family. He hadn't come for any good - he was sticking pins in the backs of the other boys, but I thought if I could get hold of him it would do good.

I always used to go to the door and shake hands with the boys, and when I got there and saw this little boy coming out, I shook hands with him, and patted him on the head. I said that I was glad to see him, and hoped he would come again.

The boy hung his head and went away, but the next night he came back and behaved better than on the previous one. He came two or three times after, and then asked us to pray for him that he might become a Christian. That was a happy night for me. He became a Christian and a good one.

Some time later, I saw the boy weeping and I wondered if his old temper had got hold of him again. He got up and I was curious as to what he would say.

"I wish you would pray for my mother," he said.

When the meeting was over I went to the boy and asked, "Have you ever spoken to your mother or tried to pray with her?"

"Well, you know, Mr. Moody," he replied, "I never had an opportunity; she doesn't believe, and won't hear me."

"Now," I said, "I want you to talk to your mother tonight. I will pray for you both."

When the boy returned home that night, he went to the sitting-room and, finding some people there, he sat waiting for an opportunity. Eventually, his mother said it was time for him to go to bed, and he went to the door undecided. He took a step, then turned around and hesitated for a minute. Then he ran to his mother and threw his arms around her neck.

"What is the matter?" she asked, thinking he was sick.

Between his sobs, the boy told his mother that for five weeks he had wanted to be a Christian. He had stopped swearing and was trying to be obedient to her. How happy he would be if she would be a Christian.

The boy went off to bed. His mother sat for a few minutes, but couldn't stand it. She went up to his room and when she got to the door, she heard him weeping and praying, "Oh, God, convert my dear mother."

She came down again, but couldn't sleep that night. Next day she told the boy to go and ask Mr. Moody to come over and see her. He called at my place of business—I was in business then—and I went over as quietly as I could.

I found her sitting in a rocking-chair weeping.

"Mr. Moody," she said, "I want to become a Christian."

"What has brought that change over you, I thought you didn't believe in it?"

Then she told me how her son had come to her, and how she hadn't slept all night, and how her sin rose up before her like a dark mountain. The next Sunday that boy came and led his mother into the Sunday School, and she became a Christian worker.

Oh, little children, if you find Christ, tell it to your fathers and mothers. Throw your arms around their necks and lead them to Jesus.

Sympathy

A few years ago, in Chicago, during July and August, many children died. I attended many funerals, sometimes as many as three a day. I got so used to it that it did not trouble me to see a mother take the last kiss and the last look at her child, and see the coffin-lid closed. I got accustomed to it, as in the war we got accustomed to the great battles, and the wounded and dead.

One night when I got home, I heard that one of my Sunday School pupils was dead, and that her mother wanted to see me. I went there and found the father drunk.

Adelaide's mother washed clothes for a living, and her daughter's work was to get wood for the fire. She had gone to the river that day and seen a piece floating on the water. She had stretched out for it, lost her balance, and fallen in.

The poor woman was very much distressed, for her husband earned no money. "I would like you to help me, Mr. Moody," she said, "to bury my child. I have no place to bury my child, and I have no money to purchase one."

Well, I took the measurements for the coffin and came away. I had my little girl,

Emma, with me and she said: "Papa, suppose we were very, very poor, and mamma had to work for a living, and I had to get sticks for the fire, and was to fall into the river, would you be very sorry?"

This question reached my heart. "Why, my child, it would break my heart to lose you," I said, and I gave her a hug.

"Papa, do you feel bad for that mother?" she said; this word woke my sympathy for the woman, and I went back to the house, and prayed that the Lord might bind up that wounded heart.

When the day came for the funeral I went to the grave yard. The drunken father was there and the poor mother. I bought a spot for the grave to be dug in and then the child was buried. There was another funeral that day, and the corpse was laid near the grave of little Adelaide. And I thought how I would feel if it had been my little girl that I had been burying there among strangers.

I went to my Sunday School thinking this, and suggested that the children should contribute some money to purchase a special grave yard for the children. We soon got it, and the papers had scarcely been made out when a lady came and said, "Mr. Moody, my little girl died this morning; let me bury her in the place that the Sunday school children bought."

The request was granted, and she asked me to go to the grave—it was a beautiful day in June, and I remember asking her what the name of her child was. She said Emma. That was the name of my little girl, and I thought what if it had been my own child.

We should put ourselves in the places of others. I could not help shedding a tear. Another woman came shortly after and wanted to burry her son there also. I asked his name. It was Willie, and it happened to be the name of my little boy—the first two laid there were called by the same names as my two children, and I felt sympathy and compassion for those two women.

If you want to be sympathetic, put yourself into other people's places. We need Christians whose hearts are full of compassion and sympathy. If we haven't got it, pray that we may have it, so that we may be able to reach those men and women that need kindly words and kindly actions, far more than sermons. The mistake is that we have been preaching too much and sympathizing too little. The gospel of Jesus Christ is a gospel of deeds and not of words.

Looking down from Heaven

When I was in Dublin I spoke about Heaven, I said that "perhaps at this moment a mother is looking down from Heaven upon her daughter here tonight," and I pointed down to a young lady in the audience. Next morning I received this letter from a father who had been there:

"On Wednesday, when you were speaking of Heaven, you said, 'It may be this moment there is a mother looking down from heaven expecting the salvation of her child who is here.' You were apparently looking at the very spot where my child was sitting. My heart said, 'that is my child. That is her mother.'

"Tears sprang to my eyes. I bowed my head and prayed, 'Lord, direct that word to my darling child's heart; Lord, save my child.' I was then anxious till the close of the meeting, when I went to her. She was bathed in tears. She rose, put her arms round me, and kissed me. When walking down to you she told me it was that same remark (about the mother looking down from heaven) that found the way home to her, and asked me, 'Papa, what can I do for Jesus?'"

The Fatal Slumber

A father took his little child out into the field one Sunday and, it being a hot day, he lay down under a beautiful shady tree. The little child ran about gathering wild flowers and little blades of grass, and coming to his father and saying, "Pretty, pretty!"

In time, the father fell asleep, and while he was sleeping the little child wandered away. When he awoke, his first thought was, "Where is my child?" He looked all around, but he could not see him. He shouted at the top of his voice, but all he heard was the echo of his own voice.

Running to a little hill the father looked around and shouted again. No response! Then going to a cliff, he looked down, and there, upon the rocks and briars, he saw the mangled form of his loved child. While he was sleeping his child had wandered over the precipice. I thought as I heard that, what a picture of the church of God!

How many fathers and mothers, how many Christian men, are sleeping now while their children wander over the terrible cliff right into the bottomless pit. Father, where is your boy tonight?

Love in the Sunday School

Mr. John Wannamaker, Superintendent of probably one of the largest Sunday schools in the world, had a theory that he would never put a boy out of his school for bad conduct. He argued, that if a boy misbehaved himself, it was through bad training at home, and that if he put him out of the school no one would take care of him.

Well, this theory was put to the test one day. A teacher came to him and said, "I've got a boy in my class who must be taken out; he breaks the rules continually, he swears and uses obscene language, and I cannot do anything with him."

Mr. Wannamaker did not care about putting the boy out, so he sent the teacher back to his class. But he came again and said that unless the boy was taken from his class, he would leave. Well, he left, and a second teacher was appointed. The second teacher came with the same story, and met with the same reply from Mr. Wannamaker. And he resigned. A third teacher was appointed, and he came with the same story as the others. Mr Wannamaker then thought he would be compelled to turn the boy out at last.

One day, a few teachers were standing about, and Mr. Wannamaker said: "I will bring this boy up and read his name out in the school, and publicly excommunicate him."

Well, a young lady came up and said to him: "I am not doing what I might for Christ; let me have the boy; I will try and save him."

But Mr. Wannamaker said: "If these young men cannot do it, you will not."

The young lady begged to have him, and Mr. Wannamaker at last consented.

She was a wealthy young lady, surrounded with all the luxuries of life. The boy went to her class, and for several Sundays he behaved himself and broke no rule. But one Sunday he broke one, and, in reply to something the teacher said, spat in her face. She took out her pocket-handkerchief and wiped her face, but she said nothing. Well, she came up with a plan, and she said to him, "John," — we will call him John, - "John, come home with me."

"No," says he, "I won't: I won't be seen on the streets with you."

She was fearful of losing him altogether if he went out of the school that day, and she said to him, "Will you let me walk home with you?"

"No I won't" said he; "I won't be seen on the streets with you."

So she came upon another plan. She said, "I won't be at home tomorrow or Tuesday, but if you will come round to the front door on Wednesday morning there will be a little bundle for you."

"I don't want it; keep your bundle."

The young lady went home and made the bundle up. She thought that curiosity might make him come.

Wednesday morning arrived and the boy thought he would just like to see what was in that bundle. The little fellow knocked at the door, which was opened, and he told his story. She said: "Yes, here is the bundle." The boy opened it and found a vest and a coat and other clothing, and a little note written by the young lady, which read something like this:

"Dear JOHNNIE: — Ever since you have been in my class I have prayed for you every morning and evening, that you might be a good boy, and I want you to keep attending my class. Do not leave me."

The next morning, before she was up, the servant came to her and said there was a little boy below who wished to see her. She dressed hastily, and went down stairs, and found Johnnie on the sofa weeping. She put her arms around his neck, and he said to her, "My dear teacher, I have not had any peace since I got this note from you. I want you to forgive me."

"Won't you let me pray for you to come to Jesus?" replied the teacher; and she went down on her knees and prayed.

Mr. Wannamaker says that Johnnie is the best boy in his Sunday school now. And so it was love that won that boy's heart.

A little quote

Many people wonder why it is that they don't prosper and are not blessed in the world. It is no wonder to me. The wonder is that God blesses them as He does. If I had a child in constant rebellion toward me, I wouldn't want the child to prosper until that spirit of rebellion was swept away, because prosperity would ruin them.

A Sad Story

There was an Englishman who had an only son; and only sons are often petted, and spoilt. This boy became very stubborn and headstrong, and very often he and his father would argue. One day they had a quarrel, and both the father and son were very angry. The father said that he wished the boy would leave home and never come back. The boy said he would go, and would not come into his father's house again till he sent for him, and the father replied that he would never send for him.

Well, away went the boy. But when a father gives up a boy, a mother does not. You mothers will understand that, but the fathers may not. You know there is no love on earth so strong as a mother's love. A great many things may separate a man and his wife; a great many things may separate a father from his son; but there is nothing in the wide world that can ever separate a true mother from her child. A true mother would never cast off her boy.

Well, the mother began to write and plead with the boy to write to his father first, and he would forgive him; but the boy said, "I will never go home till father asks me."

Then she begged the father, but he said, "No, I will never ask him."

At last the mother came down to her sick-bed, broken-hearted, and when she was given up by the physicians to die, the husband, anxious to gratify her last wish, wanted to know if there was anything he could do for her before she died. The mother gave him a look; he knew well what it meant. Then she said, "Yes, there is one thing you can do. You can send for my boy. That is the only wish on earth you can gratify. If you do not pity him and love him when I am dead and gone, who will?"

"Well," said the father, "I will send word to him that you want to see him."

"No," she said, "you know he will not come for me. If ever I see him you must send for him."

At last the father went to his office and wrote a dispatch in his own name, asking the boy to come home. As soon as the boy got the invitation from his father, he started off to see his dying mother. When he opened the door to go in he found his mother dying, and his father by the bedside.

The father heard the door open, and saw the boy, but instead of going to meet him, he went to another part of the room, and refused to speak to him. The mother kissed her son and begged him, "Now, my son, just speak to your father. You speak first, and it will all be over."

But the boy said, "No, Mother, I will not speak to him until he speaks to me."

She took her husband's hand in one of her hands and the boy's in the other, and spent her dying moments in trying to bring about a reconciliation Then just as she was about to die — she could not speak — so she put the hand of the wayward boy into the hand of the father, and passed away!

The boy looked at the mother, and the father at the wife, and at last the father's heart broke, and he opened his arms, and took that boy to his heart, and by that body they were reconciled. Sinner, that is only a faint type, a poor illustration of the reconciliation between sinners and God. This is because God is not angry with you. He is not stubborn and angry like the father was with the son. He is longing to forgive.

I bring you tonight to the dead body of Christ. I ask you to look at the wounds in his hands and feet, and the wound in his side. And I ask you, "Will you not be reconciled to God, your Heavenly Father?"

Willie and the Bean

I said to my little family, one morning, a few weeks before the Chicago fire, "I am coming home this afternoon to give you a ride."

My little boy clapped his hands. "Oh, Papa, will you take me to see the bears in Lincoln Park?"

"Yes."

You know boys are very fond of seeing bears, and I had not been gone long when my little boy said, "Mamma, I wish you would get me ready."

"Oh," she said, "it will be a long time before papa comes."

"But I want to get ready, Mamma."

At last he was ready to have the ride, face washed, and clothes all nice and clean.

"Now, you must take good care and not get yourself dirty again," said mamma.

Oh, of course he was going to take care; he wasn't going to get dirty. So off he ran to watch for me. It was a long time yet until the afternoon, and after a little he began to play. When I got home, I found him outside, with his face all covered with dirt. "I can't take you to the Park that way, Willie," I said.

"Why, Papa? You said you would take me."

"Ah, but I can't; you're covered in mud. I couldn't be seen with such a dirty little boy."

"Why, I am clean, Papa. Mamma washed me."

"Well, you've got dirty since."

My son began to cry, and I could not convince him that he was dirty. 'I am clean. Mamma washed me !" he cried.

Do you think I argued with him? No. I just took him up in my arms, and carried him into the house, and showed him his face in the mirror. He had not a word to say. He could not take my word for it; but one look at the mirror was enough; he saw it for himself: he didn't say he wasn't dirty after that!

Now the looking-glass showed him that his face was dirty— but I did not take the looking-glass to wash it; of course not. Yet that is just what thousands of people do. The law is the looking glass to see ourselves in, to show us how vile and worthless we are in the sight of God; but they take the law and try to wash themselves with it. It is only Jesus Christ who can cleanse us from sin through his death for us on the cross.

The Recitation

I heard of a Sunday School concert at which a little child of eight was going to recite. Her mother had taught her, and when the night came the little girl was trembling so much that she could scarcely speak. She commenced, "Jesus said," and completely broke down. Again she tried it: "Jesus said suffer," but she stopped once more. A third attempt was made by her, "Suffer little children — and don't anybody stop them, for He wants them all to come," and that is the truth.

If you have parents in the church remember this. God doesn't just want your parents he wants you too. If any child comes to Christ, parents or no parents, he will never turn any away who come to him. If you bring your children to God and ask the Son of God to bless them, if you train them in the knowledge of God and teach them as you walk in God's way they will be blessed.

The Blind Child

I was in an infirmary not long ago, and a mother brought a little child in. She said, "Doctor, my child's eyes have not opened for several days, can you do something for them." The doctor got some ointment and put it first on one and then on the other, and just pulled them open. "Your child is blind," said the doctor; "she will never see again."

The mother couldn't take it in. "You don't mean to say that my child will never see again?"

"Yes," replied the doctor, "your child has lost her sight, and will never see again."

The mother screamed, and hugged her child "Oh my darling," sobbed the woman, "You will never see me again. You will never see the world!"

I cried when I saw the terrible agony of that woman. It was a terrible calamity, to be in darkness; never to look upon the bright sky, the green fields; never to see the faces of loved ones; but what was it in comparison to the loss of a soul? I would rather have my eyes plucked out of my head and go down to my grave in total blindness than lose my soul.

The Child and the Atheist

I remember hearing of a Sunday School teacher who had led every one of her pupils to Christ. She was a faithful teacher. Then she tried to get her children to go out and bring other children into the school.

One day one of the children came and said she had been trying to get the children of a family to come to the school, but the father was an atheist, and he wouldn't allow it.

"What is an atheist?" asked the child. She had never heard of one before.

The teacher went on to tell her, and she was perfectly shocked.

A few mornings after, the girl happened to be going past the Post Office on her way to school, and she saw the father coming out. She went up to him and said, "Why don't you love Jesus?"

If it had been a man who had said that to him, he would probably have knocked him down. He looked at her and walked on. A second time she put the question, "Why don't you love Jesus?" He put out his hand to move her gently away from him, but looking down, he saw her tears.

"Please, sir, tell me why you don't love Jesus?"

He pushed her aside and away he went.

When he got to his office the man couldn't get this question out of his mind. "Why don't you love Jesus? Why don't you love Jesus? Why don't you love Jesus?" Everywhere he went a voice continually asked him, "Why don't you love Jesus?"

He thought that when night came and he got home with his family, he would forget it; but he couldn't. He complained that he wasn't well, and went to bed. But when he laid his head on the pillow that voice kept whispering, "Why don't you love Jesus?" He couldn't sleep.

By and by, at about midnight, he got up and said, "I will get a Bible and find where Christ contradicts himself, and then I'll have a reason," and he turned to the book of John. My friends, if you want a reason for not loving Christ, don't turn to John. He knew Him too long (I don't believe a man can read the gospel of John without being turned to Christ). Well, he read through, and found no reason why he shouldn't love Jesus, but he found many reasons why he should. He read this book, and before morning he was on his knees, and the question put by that little child led to his conversion.

The Boy who went West

A number of years ago, before any railway came into Chicago, they used to bring in the grain from the Western prairies in wagons for hundreds of miles, so as to have it shipped off on the lakes. There was a father who had a large farm out there, and who used to preach the gospel as well as attend to his farm. One day, when church business engaged him, he sent his son to Chicago with grain. He waited and waited for his boy to return, but he did not come home. At last he could wait no longer, so he saddled his horse and rode to the place where his son had sold the grain.

The farmer found that his son had been there and got the money for his grain; then he began to fear that his boy had been murdered and robbed. At last, with the aid of a detective, they tracked him to a gambling den, where they found that he had gambled away the whole of his money. In hopes of winning it back again, he had then sold his team of horses and lost that money too. He had fallen among thieves, and like the man who was going to Jericho, they stripped him, and then they cared no more about him.

What could he do? He was ashamed to go home to meet his father, and he fled. The father knew what it all meant. He knew his son expected him to be very angry. He was grieved to think that his son should have such feelings toward him. That is just exactly like the sinner. He thinks because he has sinned, God will have nothing to do with him. But what did that father do? Did he say, "Let the boy go?" No; he went after him. He arranged his business, and started after the boy. That man went from town to town, from city to city. He would get the ministers to let him preach, and at the close he would tell his story. "I have a boy who is a wanderer on the face of the earth somewhere." He would describe his boy, and say, "If you ever hear of him or see him, will you write to me?"

At last the farmer found that his son had gone to California, thousands of miles away. Did that father say, "Let him go?" No; off he went to the Pacific coast, seeking the boy. He went to San Francisco, and advertised in the newspapers that he would preach at such a church on such a day. When he had preached, he told his story in hope that the boy might have seen the advertisement and come to the church.

When he had finished, a young man seated under the gallery waited until the audience had gone out and then came towards the pulpit. The father looked and saw it was his son, and he ran to him, and lovingly embraced him. The boy wanted to confess what he had done, but not a word would the father hear. He forgave him freely, and took him to his home once more.

I tell you Christ will welcome you this minute if you will come. May God lead you to take this step. There has not been a day since you left Him that Jesus has not followed you.

A Mother Dies that her Boy may Live

When the California gold rush broke out, a man went to California, leaving his wife and son in New England. As soon as he was successful, he was to send for them. It was a long time, but at last he got enough money. The wife's heart leaped with joy. She took her boy to New York, got on board a steamer, and sailed away to San Francisco.

They had not been long at sea before the cry of "Fire! Fire!" rang through the ship. There was gun powder on board, and the Captain knew that the moment the fire reached the powder, every man, woman, and child would die.

They got out the lifeboats, but they were too small! The last one was just pushing away, when the mother pleaded with them to take her and her boy.

"No," they said, "we have got as many as we can hold."

At last they said they would take one more. Do you think she leaped into that boat and left her son to die? No! She seized her boy, gave him one last hug, kissed him, and dropped him over into the boat. "My boy," she said "if you live to see your father, tell him I died in your place."

This is a faint illustration of what Christ has done for us. He laid down his life for us. He died that we might live. Now will you love Him? What would you say of that young man if he spoke badly of his mother after what she did for him? She went down to a watery grave to save her son. Well, will you speak badly of your Saviour? May God make us loyal to Christ! My friends, you will need Him one day.

Dinna ye Hear Them Comin'?

There is a story told of an incident that occurred during the last Indian mutiny. The English were besieged in the city of Lucknow, and were afraid of being killed by those who surrounded them.

There was a little Scottish lassie in this fort, and, while lying on the ground, she suddenly shouted, her face aglow with joy, "Dinna ye hear them comin?"

"Hear what?" they asked.

"Dinna ye hear them comin'?" And she sprang to her feet.

It was the bagpipes of her native Scotland she heard being played by a regiment of her countrymen. They were marching to the relief of the captives to set them free. Oh, my friends, don't you hear Jesus Christ crying to you tonight?

Parting Words

A Christian father's little boy was sick. When he went home his wife was weeping, and she said, "Our boy is dying; he has had a change for the worse. I wish you would go in and see him."

The father went into the room and placed his hand upon the brow of his dying son, and could feel the cold, damp sweat that was gathering there. "Do you know, my boy, that you are dying?" asked the father.

"Am I? Do you really think I am dying?"

"Yes, my son, your end on earth is near."

"And will I be with Jesus tonight, father?"

"Yes, you will be with the Saviour."

"Father, don't weep, for when I get there I will go straight to Jesus and tell him that you tried all my life to lead me to Him."

God has given me two children, and ever since I can remember, I have directed them to Christ, and I would rather they carried this message to Jesus —that I had tried all my life to lead them to Him—than have all the crowns of the earth. I would rather lead them to Jesus than give them the wealth of the world. I challenge any man to speak of heaven without speaking of children. "For of such is the kingdom of heaven."

The Little Greyhound
in the Lion's Cage

A man over in Manchester had a little greyhound that he was training for a race. He had a large bet on the dog. It was a large bet considering he was such a poor man and he was anxious his dog should succeed.

The day came and the dog didn't run at all. And the owner was so mad that he beat the little greyhound and pushed it through a cage in which there was a lion. He fully expected to see the dog eaten, but the little greyhound ran right up to the lion as though it wanted mercy. Instead of the lion eating the dog, it began to lap the creature.

By and by, the man called to the dog to come out, but he wouldn't come. Then he put his hand in and the lion began to growl, and he took it out again. Some people went and told the keeper what the man had done and how he had ill-used the little greyhound. And when the keeper came, the man asked him to retrieve his dog.

The keeper asked the man how the dog got in there, but the man was too ashamed to tell. At last the keeper said, "You put him in; you'd better go and get him out; I won't do it for you." And so the dog has remained there ever since.

Now that may be a homely illustration, but I hope it will fasten on our minds the idea that we are no match for Satan. He has had six thousand years experience. I always tremble when I hear a man talk about defying Satan, and I want to add "By the grace of God" for that is the only way. Jesus Christ, who is called, The Lion of the tribe of Judah, will take care of us if we will come to him.

Off for America

When I was in London I bought a ticket to Manchester to say goodbye to some friends. When I got to the railway carriage I saw little groups of boys around another little boy who had a threadbare coat and patches all over his clothes. His mother, too poor to send him away in fine style, was obviously trying her best to make him as neat as she could.

The boy belonged to a Sunday School in London, and the group around him were his schoolmates, who had come down to say goodbye. They shook hands, and then their Sunday School teacher did the same, and wished the boy well. After that the minister came and took him by the hand and prayed that he would be blessed. When they had all said goodbye, a poor widow came up and put her arm around her son and he put his arms around her, and she began to weep.

"Don't cry, Mother," said the boy, don't cry; I'll soon be in America, and I'll save money, and soon send for you to come out to me; I'll have you out with me. Don't cry." He stepped into the carriage, the steam was turned on, and the train was in motion when he put his head out of the window and cried: "Goodbye, Mother;" and the mother's prayer went out: "God bless my boy."

Don't you think that when he arrived in America and sent the first letter to England that his mother would run quickly to the door when the postman came. How quickly she would take that letter and break the seal. She wants to hear good news. We all have a message of good news, better news than was ever received from America. It is good news from a loving Saviour—glad tidings of great joy.

Breaking the Tumblers

A lady was in her pantry and was surprised by the ringing of a bell. As she whirled around to see what it was, she broke a tumbler. Her little child was standing there, and thought her mother was doing a very good thing, and as soon as the lady left the pantry, the child commenced to break all the tumblers she could get hold of.

You may laugh, but children are very good imitators. If you don't want them to break the day of rest, keep it holy yourself. It is very often by imitation that children blaspheme, or tell a lie. When they try to quit the habit, it has grown so strong that they cannot do it.

Hold Up Your Light

A man was walking along a street one night, and saw a man with a lantern. The man seemed to be blind so he asked, "My friend, are you blind?"

"Yes," he replied

"Then why do you have a lantern?"

"I carry it so that people may not stumble over me, of course," said the man.

Learn from that blind man. Hold up your light, burning with the clear radiance of heaven so men may not stumble over you.

The Cross

At a convention in Illinois an old man got up. He said he remembered one thing about his father. He could not remember his death or his funeral, but he recollected his father one winter night, taking a little piece of wood, and with his pocket knife whittling out a little cross. He told of how God in His infinite love sent His Son down here to redeem us; how He had died on the cross for us.

The story of the cross had followed the man through life; and I tell you, if you teach children truths, they will follow them.

"A Little Child Shall Lead Them."

At a church meeting a little child was seen to be talking so earnestly to a companion, that a lady sat down by her to hear what she was saying. She found that the child was telling her friend how much Jesus loved her, and how she loved him, and was asking her little companion if she would love him too.

The lady was so impressed by these words that she spoke to an anxious soul that night for the first time in her life. And so "a little child shall lead them."

The Child and the Book

I like to think of Christ as a burden bearer. A minister was one day moving his library upstairs. His son came in and was anxious to help him. The minister told him to go and get an armful and take them upstairs.

When the boy's father came back, he met the little fellow crying on the stairs. He had been tugging away at the biggest book in the library, but just hadn't managed to carry it up. The minister took his son in his arms, book and all, and carried him upstairs. So Christ will carry you and all your burdens.

A little quote

Let me say, find some work.
See if you can get a Sunday
School to teach, and if you cannot,
find other opportunities.
When you have won one soul to
Christ, you will want to win two,
and when you get into the luxury of
winning souls it will be a new
world to you.

The Horse that was Established

A little boy was converted and he was full of praise. When God converts someone, that person's heart is full of joy and can't help praising. Well, the boy's father was a professed Christian, and his son wondered why he didn't talk about Christ, and didn't go down to the special meetings.

One day, as the father was reading the papers, the boy came to him and put his hand on his shoulder and said: "Why don't you praise God? Why don't you sing about Christ? Why don't you go down to these meetings that are being held?"

The father looked at him and said, gruffly: "I am not carried away with any of these doctrines. I am established."

A few days later, they were getting out a load of wood and put it on the cart. They climbed on top of the wood and tried to get the horse to go. The whip was cracked, but the animal refused to budge. They tried to roll the wagon along, but without success.

"I wonder what's the matter?" said the father.

"He's established," replied the boy.

You may laugh at that, but this is the way with a good many Christians.

Dr. Chalmer's Story

There is a story of a Dr. Chalmers. A lady came to him one day and said: "Doctor, I cannot bring my child to Christ. I've talked, and talked, but it's of no use."

The doctor said, "Don't worry, I will talk to her alone."

When he saw the girl, he said to her, "They are bothering you a good deal about God and Jesus Christ; now suppose I just tell your mother you don't want to be talked to any more upon this subject for a year. How will that do?"

Well, the lassie hesitated a little, and then said she "I don't think it would be safe to wait for a year. Something might turn up. I might die before then."

"Well, that's so," replied the doctor, "but suppose we say six months."

She didn't think that this would be safe either.

"That's so," was the doctor's reply; "well, let us say three months."

After a little hesitation, the girl finally said, "I don't think it would be safe to put it off for three months—I don't think it would be safe to put it off at all," and they went down on their knees and found Christ.

Johnny, Cling Close to the Rock

Little Johnny and his sister were going through a long, narrow railroad tunnel one day. The railroad company had built small clefts here and there through the tunnel, so that if any one got caught in it when the train was passing, they could save themselves.

After the little boy and girl had gone some distance in the tunnel, they heard a train coming. They were frightened at first, but the sister put her brother in one cleft and then hurried for shelter in another. The train came thundering along, and as it passed, the sister cried out: "Johnny, cling close to the rock Johnny, cling close to the rock," and they were safe.

The "Rock of Ages" may be beaten by the storms and waves of trouble, but "cling close to the rock, Christians, and all will be well." The waves don't touch the Christian; he is sheltered by the Rock "that is higher than I," by the One who is the strong arm, and the Saviour who is mighty and willing to save.

Obedience Explained

Suppose I say to my boy, "Willie, I want you to go out and bring me a glass of water," and he says he doesn't want to go.

"I didn't ask you whether you wanted to go or not, Willie; I told you to go."

"But I don't want to go," he says.

"You must get me a glass of water."

He does not like to go. But he knows I like grapes, and he likes them too, so he goes out, and gets a beautiful cluster of grapes. He returns and says, "Papa, here is a beautiful cluster of grapes for you."

"But what about the water?"

"Won't the grapes be acceptable, Papa?"

"No, the grapes are not acceptable; I want you to get me a glass of water."

The little fellow doesn't want to get the water, but he goes out, and this time someone gives him an orange. He brings it in and places it before me. "Is that acceptable?" he asks.

"No, no, no!" I say; "I want nothing but water; you cannot do anything to please me until you get the water."

And so, my friends, to please God you must first obey Him.

Jumping into Father's Arms

I was attending meetings in a place called Mobile when something happened which I will tell you about. It was a beautiful evening, and just before the meeting some neighbours and myself were sitting on the front porch enjoying the evening.

One of the neighbours put a child of his upon a ledge eight feet high, and put out his hands and told him to jump. Without the slightest hesitation he sprang into his father's arms. Another child was lifted up, and he, too, readily sprang into the arms of his father.

The man picked up another boy, larger than the others, and held out his arm, but he wouldn't jump. He cried and screamed to be taken down. The man begged the boy to jump, but it was of no use; he couldn't be persuaded to do it.

The incident made me curious, and I stepped up to him and asked, "How was it that those two little fellows jumped so readily into your arms and the other boy wouldn't?"

"Why," said the man, "those two boys are my children and the other boy isn't, he doesn't know me."

The Miner and his Children

When I was holding meetings a little time ago at Wharnecliff, a coal district in England, a burly miner came up to me and said in his Yorkshire dialect, "Dost know wha was at meetin' t'night?" (Do you know who was at the meeting tonight?)

"No," I answered.

He mentioned a familiar name — a very bad man, one of the wildest, wickedest men in Yorkshire.

"Well," said the man, "he came into meetin' an' said you didn't preach right; he said you preach nothin' but the love o' Christ, an' that won't do for drunken miners; you must shake 'em over a pit, and he says he'll ne'er come again."

What this man meant was that he thought I didn't preach about hell. Mark you, my friends, I believe in hell, the pit that burns, and the fire that's never quenched but I believe that the magnet that goes down to the bottom of the pit is the love of Jesus.

I didn't expect to see this wild man again, but he came straight from the coal mine the next night, without washing his face, and with all his working clothes upon him. He sat down, drunk, on one of the seats that were used for the children, and got as near to me as possible.

The sermon was all about the love of Jesus Christ. He listened at first attentively, but by-and-by I saw him using the sleeve of his rough coat to wipe his eyes. Soon after we had an inquiry meeting, when some of those praying miners got around him, and it wasn't long before he was crying, "Oh, Lord, save me; I am lost; Jesus have mercy upon me," and he left that meeting a new creature.

His wife told me herself; what occurred when he came home. His little children heard him coming along—they knew the step of his heavy clogs—and ran to their mother in terror, clinging to her skirts. He had had a habit of banging the door, but this time he opened it as gently as could be. When he came into the house and saw the children clinging to their mother, frightened, he just stooped down, picked up the youngest girl in his arms, and looked at her with the tears rolling down his cheeks.

"Mary, God has sent your father home to you," he said, and kissed her. He picked up another, "God has sent your father home;" and from one to another he went, and kissed them all. Then he came to his wife and put his arms around her neck,

"Don't cry, lass; don't cry. God has sent your husband home at last; don't cry," and all she could do was to put her arms around his neck and sob.

The miner said: "Have you got a Bible in the house, lass?" They hadn't such a thing.

"Well, lass, if we haven't we must pray."

They got down on their knees, and all he could say was:

"Gentle Jesus, meek and mild,

Look upon a little child;

Pity my simplicity

— for Jesus Christ's sake, amen."

It was a simple prayer, but God answered it. While I was at Barnet some time after that, a friend came to me and said: "I've got good news for you." and he went on to tell us that this miner, so recently converted to Christ, was preaching the gospel everywhere he went—in the coal mine, and out of the coal mine. "He is trying to win everybody to the Lord Jesus Christ."

Work Among the Street Children

There is a wealthy gentleman in London who has done a great deal of good. He would go down to the Seven Dials, one of the worst places in London. He would stay till two in the morning, helping street children, and taking them into the house of shelter. He spent thousands of pounds in that part of London.

Over 300 young men, whom he had brought from the slums are now in China, Australia, and some in America.

When he took them in he would have their photographs taken in their rags and dirt. Then they were given a bath and new clothes. They were put into an institution, taught a trade, and not only the rules of life but every one of them was taught to read his Bible. After a few years of care and education, before they left, they were taken to a photograph gallery where their picture was taken. Both photographs were then given to them. This was to show them the condition in which the institution found them, and that in which it left them. So, my friends, remember where God found you.

Found in the Sand

While I was attending a meeting some time ago, a lady, who has since died, came to me and said: "I want you to come home with me; I have something to say to you."

When we reached her home, she put her arms on the table, and tears came into her eyes, but with an effort she repressed her emotion. After a struggle she went on to say that she was going to tell me something that she had never told any other living person.

She said she had a son in Chicago, and she was very anxious about him. When he was young he got interested in religion at the rooms of the Young Men's Christian Association. He used to go out in the street and circulate tracts. He was her only son, and she was very ambitious that he should make a name in the world, and wanted him to get into the very highest circles.

Oh, what a mistake people make about these highest circles. Society is false; it is a sham. She was deceived like a good many more followers of fashion and hunters after wealth at the present time. She thought it was beneath her son to associate with young men who hadn't much money. She tried to get him away from them, but they had more influence than she had, and, finally, to break his whole association, she packed him off to a boarding school.

He went soon to Yale College, and she supposed he got into one of those miserable secret societies there that have ruined so many young men, and the next thing she heard was that the boy had gone astray. She began to write letters, urging him to come into the Kingdom of God; but she heard that he tore the letters up without reading them. She went to him to try and regain whatever influence she possessed over him, but her efforts were useless, and she came home with a broken heart.

The boy left New Haven, and for two years they heard nothing of him. At last they discovered that he was in Chicago, and his father found him and gave him $30,000 to start in business. They thought it would change him, but it didn't. They asked me, when I went back to Chicago, to try and use my influence with him.

I got a friend to invite the boy to his house one night, where I intended to meet him, but he heard I was to be there and did not come. Like a good many other young men he seemed to be afraid of me. I tried many times to reach him, but could not.

While I was travelling one day on the New Haven Railroad, I bought a New York paper, and in it I saw a dispatch saying he had been drowned in Lake Michigan. His father came down to find his body, and after considerable searching, they discovered it. All his clothes and his body were covered with sand. The body was taken home to his broken-hearted mother. She said, "If I thought he was in heaven I would have peace."

Her disobedience of God's law came back upon her. So, my friends, if you have a boy interested in the gospel, help him to come to Christ.

The Little Norwegian

I remember while in Boston I attended one of the daily prayer meetings. The meetings we had been holding had been almost always taken by young men. Well, in that meeting a little Norwegian boy stood up. He could hardly speak a word of English, but he got up and came to the front. He trembled all over and the tears were trickling down his cheeks, but he spoke out as well as he could and said: "If I tell the world about Jesus, then he will tell the Father about me." He then took his seat. That was all he said.

I tell you that in those few words he said more than all of them, old and young together. Those few words went straight down into the heart of everyone present. "If I tell the world " — yes, that's what it means to confess Christ.

For Charlie's Sake

One day a minister was telling about the mighty power Christians call on for help when they say, "for Christ's sake!" or "in Jesus' name!" and he told a story that made a great impression on me.

When the war came on, he said, his only son left for the army, and he suddenly became interested in soldiers. Every soldier that passed by reminded him of his son. He went to work for soldiers. When he met a sick soldier one day, so weak he couldn't walk, he took him in a carriage, and got him into the Soldiers' Home.

Soon, he became President of the Soldiers' Home in Columbus, and used to go down everyday and spend hours looking after those soldiers, and seeing that they were comfortable. He spent a great deal of time and money on them.

One day, the man said to his wife, "I'm giving too much time to these soldiers, I've got to stop it. I've got to attend to my own business." So he went to the office resolved in future to leave the soldiers alone. He went to his desk, and started writing.

Pretty soon the door opened, and he saw a soldier hobble slowly in. He got a fright at the sight of him. The man was fumbling at something in his pocket, and he got out an old soiled paper. The father saw it was his own son's writing.

"DEAR FATHER, This young man belongs to my company. He has lost his leg and his health in defence of his country, and he is going home to his mother to die. If he calls on you treat him kindly, "FOR CHARLIE'S SAKE."

"For Charlie's sake." The moment he saw that, a pang went to his heart. He got up for a carriage, lifted the maimed soldier, drove home, put him into Charlie's room. He sent for the family physician, kept him in the family and treated him like his own son.

When the young soldier became well enough to go home to his mother, the father took him to the railway station, put him in the nicest, most comfortable place in the carriage, and sent him on his way.

"I did it," said the father, "for Charlie's sake."

Now, whatever you do, my friends, do it for the Lord Jesus' sake. Do and ask everything in His name, in the name of Him "who loved us and gave Himself for us."

A little quote

*If we make those
Bible truths interesting -
break them up in some shape
so that the children can get at them,
then they will begin to enjoy them.*

Picking up the Bible

The hardest thing, I will admit, that a man ever has to do is to become a Christian, and yet it is the easiest. This seems to many to be a contradiction, but I will repeat it, it is the most difficult thing to become a Christian, and yet it is the easiest.

I have a little nephew in Chicago. When he was three or four years of age, he threw that Bible on the floor. I think a good deal of that Bible, and I didn't like to see this.

His mother said to him, "Go pick up Uncle's Bible from the floor."

"I won't," he replied.

"Go and pick that Bible up directly."

"I won't."

"What did you say?" asked his mother. She thought he didn't understand. But he understood well enough, and had made up his mind that he wouldn't.

She told the boy she would have to punish him if he didn't, and then he said he couldn't, and by and by he said he didn't want to. And that is the way with people in coming to Christ. At first they say they won't, then they can't, and then they don't want to.

The mother insisted upon the boy

picking up the Bible, and he got down and put his arms around it and pretended he couldn't lift it. He was a great, healthy boy, and he could have picked it up easily enough. I was very anxious to see the fight carried on because she was a young mother, and if she didn't break that boy's will he was going to break her heart by and by.

She told him again that if he didn't pick it up she would punish him, and the child just picked it up. It was very easy to do it when he made up his mind.

So it is perfectly easy for men to accept the gospel. The trouble is they don't want to give up their will. If you want to be saved you must just accept that gospel — that Christ is your Saviour, that He is your Redeemer, and that He has rescued you from the curse of the law. Just say "Lord Jesus Christ, I trust you from this hour to save me;" and the moment you take that stand, He will put His loving arms around you and wrap about you the robe of righteousness.

Willie

Just after I returned to America I received a letter from Scotland.

A loving father was asking us to look out for his boy whose name was Willie. That name touched my heart, because it was the name of my own boy. I tried to track down the boy, but all efforts were fruitless.

Away off in Scotland, that Christian father was prayed to God for his boy, and last Friday, at our prayer meeting, among those asking for prayers was that Willie. This young man told me a story that thrilled my heart, and showed me that the prayers of his father and mother in that far off land had been used to bring him to Christ.

He said he was rushing madly to destruction, but there was a power in those prayers that saved him. God hears and answers prayers. We should lift up our voices to Him in prayer, that He will bless the children He has given us.

The Mistake that was Corrected

When we were in Great Britain, in Manchester, a father woke up to the fact that we were going away from that town. Just as we were about to close he became wonderfully interested in the meetings, and when we had gone to another town he said to his wife: "I have made a mistake; I should have taken you and the children and the servants to those meetings. I will take you all to the town where they are and rent a house and we can attend the meetings."

He came and rented a house and I remember him coming to me one night, soon after arriving, and saying, "Mr. Moody, my wife has been converted; thank God for that. If I get nothing else I am well paid." A few nights after he came in and said his son had become converted and one of the servants. So he went on until the last day we were to be in that town, and he came to me and said the last one of the family had yielded himself up to Christ, and he went back to his native city rejoicing.

When we were in London the father and son came and assisted in the work. I don't know a happier man in all Europe than that one.

Moody Chasing his Shadow

When I was a little boy I remember I tried to catch my shadow. I don't know if you were ever so foolish; but I remember running after it and trying to get ahead of it. I could not see why the shadow always kept ahead of me. Once I happened to be racing with my face to the sun, and I looked over my head and saw that my shadow was behind me all the way.

It is the same with the Son of Righteousness; peace and joy will go with you while you go with your face toward Him, and these people who are getting at the back of the Sun are in darkness all the time. Turn to the light of God and the reflection will flash in your heart. Don't say that God will not forgive you. It is only your will which keeps His forgiveness from you.

Open The Door

I heard of a little child some time ago who had been burned. The mother had gone out and left the three children at home. The eldest left the room, and the remaining two began to play with fire, and set the place ablaze. When the youngest of the two saw what she had done, she went into a little cupboard and fastened herself in. The remaining child went to the door and knocked and knocked, crying to her to open the door and let her take her out of the burning building, but she was too frightened to do it.

It seems to me as if this was the way with hundreds and thousands. Christ stands and knocks, but they've got their hearts barred and bolted, because they don't know that He has come only to bless them.

Higher and Higher

I remember, a few years ago, a little child died, and just before his soul went home, he asked his father to lift him up. The father put his hand under the head of the child and raised it up, but the child only said, "That is not enough; that is not what I want; lift me right up."

The child was wasted all to skin and bones, but his father agreed, and lifted the dying child out of his bed. But the little fellow kept whispering, fainter and fainter, "Lift me higher, higher, higher!" And the father lifted higher and higher, till he lifted him as far as he could reach. Yet, still the barely audible whisper came, "Higher, father, higher," till at last, his head fell back, and his spirit passed up to the eternal King—high at last.

So let your constant cry be higher, higher, nearer the cross of the Son of God.

Believe

Have faith in God! Take Him at His word! Believe what He says! Believe what he says about His Son! I can imagine some of you saying: "I want to, but I have not got the right kind of faith." What faith do you want? The idea that you want a different kind of faith is all wrong. Use the faith you have got, just believe on the Lord Jesus Christ. You can't give any reason for not believing.

If a man told me he couldn't believe me, I would ask him why. I would have a right to ask if I had ever broken my word; and if I had not then why didn't he believe me. I would like to ask you, has God ever broken His word? Never. He will keep His word.

God condemns the world because they don't believe in Him; that is the root of all evil. A man who believes in the Lord Jesus Christ won't murder, and lie, and do all these awful things. Don't get caught up by that terrible delusion that unbelief is a misfortune. Unbelief is not a misfortune, but is the sin of the world. Christ found it on all sides of the world. When He rose from the grave, He found that his disciples doubted. He had reason to cry out against unbelief.

"Let the Lower Lights be Burning."

At the mouth of a harbour, there were two lights called the upper and lower lights; and to enter the harbour safely by night, vessels must see both of the lights.

One stormy night a captain and pilot anxiously watched for the lights. The pilot asked, "Do you see the lower light?"

"No," was the reply; "I fear we have passed them."

"Yes, there are the upper lights. We have passed the lower lights, and have lost our chance of getting into the harbour."

They looked back, and saw the dim outline of the lower lighthouse against the sky. The lights had gone out.

The storm was so bad that they could do nothing. They tried to make for the harbour, but crashed against the rocks, and sank. Few escaped. Why? Simply because the lower lights had gone out.

Christ is our upper light, and we are the lower lights, and the cry to us is, *Keep the lower lights burning*; that is what we have to do. We have to keep following Christ, to keep honouring him. We must keep our lights burning and He will lead us safe to heaven where there is no more night.

The Good Mother

A young man went home from one of our meetings some time ago. He had been converted. He had previously been a wild young man. His mother had made it a rule, she told me, that she "would not go to bed till he came home." That was her rule. If he did not come home till five o'clock in the morning, she sat up, and when he was out all night she got no sleep; but when he came home she always met him with a kiss and threw her arms around his neck. She treated him just as if he was kind, attentive and good. Sometimes he would be out all night. Those nights she would not go to bed and he knew it.

One night her son came home. She looked to see if he was under the influence of alcohol. He came up to her, and he said, 'Mother I have been converted,' and then she embraced him, and wept tears of joy. "Why," she said, "Mr. Moody, you don't know what joy it gave me. You don't know how I praised God that my prayers had been answered."

A Voice from the Tomb

The other day I read of a mother who died, leaving her child alone and very poor. While she had been alive, the mother had prayed earnestly for her boy, and left an impression upon his mind that she cared more for his soul than she cared for anything else in the world. He grew up to be a successful man in business, and became very well off.

After his mother had been dead for twenty years, the businessman thought he would remove her remains to his own lot in the cemetery, and put up a monument to her memory. As he came to remove them the thought came to him that his mother had prayed for him while she was alive, and he wondered why her prayers had not been answered. That very night the man was saved.

The act of removing her body to another resting-place reminded him of his childhood, and he become a Christian.

"Hold the Fort, For I am coming."

When General Sherman travelled through the Southern States of America, he left a handful of men guarding rations in a fort in the Kenesaw Mountains.

General Hood attacked the fort and for a long time the battle raged fearfully. Half the men were either killed or injured, and the general in command was wounded seven times. The troops were ready to surrender the fort when Sherman sent a message through a signal corps on the mountain: "Hold the fort; I am coming. W. T. Sherman." That message fired up their hearts. They held the fort till reinforcements came from fifteen miles away, and it did not go into the hands of their enemies.

As Christians we must remember that our Saviour is in command and He is coming. We are instruced to hold the fort, to keep up the fight for he is coming.

The Dying Sunday-School Teacher

I want to tell you how I got my first impulse to work only for the conversion of sinners. For a long time after my conversion I didn't accomplish anything. I hadn't thought enough about this personal work.

The change came in 1860. One of the teachers in the Sunday School was a pale, delicate, young man. I knew his ddep devotion to God and gave him the worst class in the school. They were all girls, and they kept fooling around in the school-room and disrupting the lessons, yet this young man had better success than anyone else.

One Sunday he was absent and I tried to teach the class. I couldn't do anything with them - they were completely unconcerned about their souls. Well, early the following morning the young man came to the store where I worked and, pale faced, threw himself down on some boxes.

"What's the matter?" I asked.

"I have been bleeding at the lungs, and they have said that I will die," he said.

"But you are not afraid to die?" I questioned.

"No," said he, "I am not afraid to die, but I have got to stand before God and give an account of my stewardship, and not one of my Sunday-School pupils have been brought to Jesus. I have failed to bring one, and haven't any strength to do it now."

He was so anxious that I got a carriage and we called at the homes of every one of his scholars. To each one he said as best as his faint voice would let him, "I have come to just ask you to come to the Saviour," and then he prayed as I had never heard before.

For ten days he laboured in that way, sometimes walking to the nearest houses, and at the end of that ten days every one of that large class had come to Christ.

The night before he went away (for the doctors had said that he must hurry to the South). We met together to sing and pray for him.

It was a beautiful night in June when he left and I went down to the train to help him. Every one of the Sunday school girls was gathered there and the station was a joyful, yet tearful place as we said farewell. At last the gong sounded and, supported on the platform, the dying man shook hands with each one, and whispered, "I will meet you in heaven."

A Little Bird's Freedom

A friend in Ireland once met a little Irish boy who had caught a sparrow. The poor little bird was trembling in his hand and seemed very anxious to escape. The gentleman begged the boy to let it go, but he said that he would not for he had chased it for three hours before catching it.

The gentleman tried to persuade the boy but without success. Eventually, he offered to buy the bird and the boy agreed on a price. Then the gentleman took the poor little thing and held it out in his hand. The boy had been holding it very tightly, for he was stronger than the bird.

The sparrow sat for a time, scarcely able to realize the fact that it had got liberty; but in a little while it flew away, chirping, as if to say to the gentleman, "Thank you! Thank you! You have redeemed me."

That is what redemption is — buying back and setting free. So Christ came back to break the chains of sin, to open the prison doors and set the sinner free. This is the good news, the gospel of Christ.

Finding Your Picture

I have an idea that the Bible is like an album. I go into a man's house, and while waiting for him I pick up an album and open it. I look at a picture and think, "Why, that looks like a man I know." I turn over and look at another. "Well, I know that man." By and by I come upon another. "Why, that man looks like my brother."

I am getting pretty near home. I keep turning over the leaves. "Well, I declare, there is a man who lives in the street I do — why, he is my next-door neighbour." And then I come upon another and I see myself.

My friends, if you read your Bibles you will find your own pictures there - it will just describe you. Now it may be that there is some Pharisee here tonight and if there is, let him turn to the third chapter of John and see what Christ said to that Pharisee.

"Unless a man is born again he cannot enter the kingdom of God."

Nicodemus was one of the finest specimens of a man in Jerusalem in those days, yet he had to be born again or he wouldn't see the kingdom of God. You may say: "I am not a Pharisee; I am a poor, miserable sinner who is too bad to come to

Him." Well, turn to the woman of Samaria and see what He said to her. See what a difference there was between them. The distance between them was as great as that between the sun and the moon. One was in the very highest station, and the other occupied the very worst. One had only himself and his sins to bring to God, the other was trying to bring in his high position and his aristocracy.

I tell you, when a man gets a true sight of himself, he drops all false ideas about himself. See this prayer: "I thank God, I am not like other men, - I fast, - I give, - I possess." When a man prays, to God, he does not praise himself. He falls flat in the dust before God. In that prayer you don't find him thanking God for what He had done for him. It was an unbeliever's, prayerless prayer—just going through the motions.

I hope the day will come when formal prayers will be a thing of the past. Formal Christians get up like this Pharisee and thank God they are not like other men; but when a man gets a look at himself he prays with the spirit of the publican.

A little quote

I tell you Christ will welcome you
this minute if you will come.
May God lead you
to take this step.
There has not been a day
since you left Him
that Jesus has not followed you.

The Loved one and the Lover

There are a great many things to separate a man from his wife, or one friend from another; but the mother's love is generally unchangeable. Her son may be a murderer; public opinion may be against him and the newspapers may vilify him. His friends may drop him, but his mother will take her stand in the court beside her boy. The jury may give a verdict against him, and he may be sentenced to death; but you will find that mother going down to his cell, and she will love him through it all.

She doesn't care for public opinion; she doesn't pay attention to the feelings of the world. Everything may be gone from her, but love for her son will remain. And when that son has been executed, and life has left his body, she will go down to his grave and water it with tears, and will cherish the memory of that boy as long as she lives. But all this is not to be compared with the love of God. God's love is not confined to one man; it is universal and unfailing and unchangeable.

Humility

I suppose Isaiah thought he was as good as most men in his day, and perhaps he was a good deal better than most men, but when he saw the Lord he cried, "Woe is me, for I am undone; because I am a man of unclean lips." When he saw the Lord he saw his own deformity, and he fell in the dust before the Lord. And that is the proper place for a sinner.

As I have said before, until men realise their uncleanness they talk of their own righteousness, but the moment they catch a sight of Him their mouth is stopped. If we hear a man talking about himself we may be sure that he has not seen God. Look at Daniel - not a thing could be found against him, but when he came within sight of God he found that his goodness was worthless.

Look at Job. One would have thought that he was all right. He was good to the poor, generous to all charities — not a better man within a thousand miles. If they wanted to get a thousand dollars to endow a university, a thousand dollars to build a synagogue, if they wanted a thousand dollars for any charitable object, why, he was the man. You would have liked to get him into your Presbyterian or Methodist, or

Baptist Churches and if you wanted a chairman of a benevolent society you couldn't have found a better man. Yet look at him when God came near him.

It is altogether different when God comes within our sight. It is one thing to hear Him and another thing to see Him. Job learned a lesson. No-one can come into God's kingdom till he knows that he is vile, till he sees God. We must realise that.

The Little Winner

A little girl of only eleven years old once came to me in a Sunday School and said: "Will you please pray that God will make me a winner of souls?" I felt so proud of her, and my pride was justified, for she has become one of the best winners of souls in the country. Oh, suppose she lives sixty years, and goes on winning four or five souls every year; at the end of her journey there will be three hundred souls on the way to glory. And how long will it be before that little company swells to a great army.

Don't you see how that little mountain stream keeps swelling till it carries everything before it. Little trickling streams run into it, till now it is a mighty river, with great cities on its banks, and the large boats and barges floating on its waters. So when a single soul is won to Christ you cannot see the result. A single one multiplies to a thousand, and that to ten thousand. Perhaps a million shall be the fruit; we cannot tell. We only know that the Christian who has turned so many to righteousness shall indeed shine for ever and ever.

Blind Bartimeus

The apostle is going into Jericho for the last time. By the wayside he finds a blind beggar who asks for money, and he says "silver and gold have I none, but I can tell you of a great physician in Israel who can cure you."

"Cure me?" he says "I was born blind."

"Yes, but I have talked to a man in Jerusalem who says he was born blind, but now he sees."

"Why," says Bartimeus, "how is that?"

"Well, Jesus of Nazareth was in Jerusalem, and a boy led the blind man to Him. He just made clay with spittle, anointed his eyes, and sent him to wash in the pool of Siloam. If you could only go up to Jerusalem, all you would have to do would be to tell Him. He doesn't charge anything."

"He doesn't?"

"No; He treats princes and penniless the same. You only have to ask Him."

Bartimeus cries out: "If I can get my sight just by asking, I will do it." He takes his place by the wayside in expectancy and hears someone approaching. "Who is coming?" He cries out, but no-one answers, and he begins to doubt that it is Jesus of Nazareth.

He shouts again with a louder voice, and they tell him that Jesus is passing by.

"Jesus, Son of David, have mercy upon me." he cries with all his might.

Some of the crowd think that Christ is going up to Jerusalem to be crowned King and do not want Him to be disturbed by the blind beggar. They tell him not to bother the Master; but the beggar will not give up and cries all the louder: "Son of David have mercy upon me."

The prayer reaches the ear of the Son of God, and he hushes all the voices about Him while He listens to the earnest caller. Bartimeus realises that what he heard wa true - there was no mistake.

The Bible

People say that the Bible was good enough for ancient days, but we have men of culture, of science and of literature now, and its value has decreased. Now, give me a better book and I will throw it away.

Has the world ever offered us a better book? These men want us to give up the Bible. What are you going to give us in its place? Oh, how cruel it is to tell us to give up all the hope we have—to throw away the only book which tells the story of the resurrection. They try to tell us that it is all a fiction, so that when we lay our loved ones in the grave we say goodbye to them for time and eternity.

Away with this terrible doctrine. The Bible is true. When man tries to draw us to another way, it is the work of the devil. Men say we have outgrown the Bible. Why don't they outgrow the light of the sun? They shouldn't let the light of the sun come into their buildings—they should have electricity. The sun is old, and electricity is a new light.

How much we owe the Bible. Why, I don't think human life would be safe if it wasn't for it.

Child Friendship — How Durable

I heard some time ago of a little book upon a passage of Scripture which occurred in the story of David and Mephiboseth. You know, one day when Jonathan and David are together, Jonathan says, "David, I want you to make a vow."

I suppose it had been revealed to Jonathan that David was to take his place as the new king and instead of his heart being filled with jealousy, he loves him as a brother.

"Now, I want you to make a vow that when you get my father's throne, you will show kindness to any of my father's house who are alive."

"Why, yes, Jonathan," replies David, "I will. I will do it for your sake alone."

Well, time goes on and news comes to David that the Israelites have been defeated in war, and that Saul and Jonathan are dead. David goes to Hebron and reigns for seven-and-a-half years, and then moves to Jerusalem.

I can see David in his palace during the height of his power, when the recollection of the old vow he made to Jonathan suddenly comes upon him. His conscience tells him that he has made a vow which he has not kept. I can imagine him summoning one of his servants, "Do you know if there are any of Saul's house alive?"

"Well, I don't know, but there is Ziba, an old servant of Saul's."

David summons Ziba and asks: "Are any of Saul's house alive, because if there are I want to show kindness to them."

I can imagine the expression on Ziba's face. The idea of David showing kindness to any of Saul's house — to Saul, who persecuted David and wanted him dead.

"Well, yes," the servant answers, "there is a son of Jonathan living."

"What," he cries, "a son of my old friend Jonathan. Where is he?"

"He was at Lo-debar the last I heard of him."

When David hears the news, he sends for Jonathan's son, Mephibosheth. Imagine that chariot sweeping through the town. "Why, the King's chariot is here," the people say, "What does it mean?"

We are told in the story that this poor prince is lame, and I can see him as he comes out to meet the servant.

"What is it?" he inquires.

"King David has sent for you," the servant replies.

I can see the prince trembling when he hears this. He thinks King David wants to kill him – that's the way with sinners. They think that God stands behind them with a large sword ready to destroy them.

The servant says: "I want you to come down and see the king."

"But," replies the prince, "that means death to me."

"He has sent me, and wants you to come," insists the servant, and he gets him into the carriage and on to the palace of the king.

The king looks upon Mephibosheth and sees how he looks like Jonathan. He says to Mephibosheth, "I will show you kindness for your father's sake. I will restore to you all of Saul's possessions, and you shall sit at the king's table."

He restores to the lame prince the inheritance he lost and then gives him a place at his table. That is what God wants for you . He wants you to take your inheritance. If you are a sinner, a backslider, he wants you to return to him, to come to the city of peace where you will learn the good news of God's love and salvation for you.

Son, Remember

I have been twice in the jaws of death. Once I nearly drowned, but when I was about to go under the water for a third time I was rescued. In the twinkling of an eye everything I had said, done, or thought of, flashed across my mind. I do not understand how everything in a man's life can be crowded into his recollection in an instant of time, but nevertheless it all flashed through my mind.

Another time when I thought I was dying, it all came back to me again. It is just so that all things we think we have forgotten will come back to us. It is only a question of time. We will hear the words, "Son, remember," and it is a good deal better for us now to remember our sins and confess them before it is too late.

Christ said to his disciples, "Remember Lot's wife." Over and over again, when the children of Israel were brought out of Egypt, God said to them, "Remember where I found you, and how I delivered you." He wanted them to remember His goodness to them, and the time is coming when, if they forget His goodness and despise it, they will be without mercy.

The Prodigal's Return

The young man's friends laugh at him, but what does he care for public opinion. "I have made up my mind," he says. He doesn't stay to get a new suit of clothes as some men do in coming to Christ. They want to do some good deeds before they come. He just started as he was.

I see him walking on dusty roads and over hills, and crossing brooks and rivers. It didn't take him long to go home when he'd made up his mind.

Going home after being away for a few months you long to catch a glimpse of that old place. As you near it you remember the precious hours and the pleasant days of childhood.

As the prodigal comes near his old home; all his days of happy childhood come before him. He wonders if his father is still alive, and as he comes near the home he says: "It may be that he is dead." Ah! what a sad thing it would have been if he found that his father had died mourning for him.

Is there anyone here who has a father and mother, whose love you are scorning and to whom you have not written for years? I said to a prodigal the other night, "How long is it since you have written to your mother?"

"Four and a half years."

"Don't you believe your mother loves you?"

"Yes," he replied, "it is because she loves me that I don't write. If I told her the life I've been leading, it would break her heart."

"If you love her," I said, "go and write to her tonight and tell her all."

I got his promise, and I am happy. I can't tell how glad I am when young prodigals return home. I know how joyful their parents will be when they hear from them.

As our prodigal son nears his father's home, he wonders if the man's heart will have turned against him. Will he receive a welcome? He doesn't know his father's heart. The old man is up there on that flat roof, in the cool of the day, waiting for his boy. He has been there every day, straining his eyes to catch the first glimpse of his son, should he return. He is still there hoping to see the wanderer come back. He sees a form in the distance, and as it comes nearer, he can tell that it is a young man. He cannot tell who it is by his dress. His robe is gone, and his ring and shoes too, but the old man catches sight of the face.

He comes running down, his long white hair floating through the air. He rushes past his servants, out of the door, and up to his son, whom he warmly embraces. He rejoices over him.

The young man tries to make a speech— he tries to ask his father if he can be one of his servants, but the father won't listen to it. When he gets him to the house he cries to one servant, "Go and get the best robe for him;" and to another, "You go and get a ring and put it on his finger," He tells other servants to fetch his son some shoes and to kill the fatted calf.

There was joy there. "My boy who was dead is alive again." There was joy in that house.

The Ivan Series

Ivan and the Informer
Ivan is at a secret bible study but when he leaves someone is waiting outside - the secret police. How did they find out about the study? What should Ivan do? Find out how Ivan tackles the police, false accusations and the usual problems with spiteful schoolmates.

Ivan and the Hidden Bible
Ivan and Katya are at the Lenin Collective Farm to help with the harvest. All Ivan's class are there and Ivan and Katya can't wait to start work. But they have something else on their minds. There is a hidden bible on the farm, one that used to belong to Ivan and Katya's grandfather. Can they find it?

Ivan and the Secret in the Suitcase
Ivan has been asked to take part in a dangerous mission. While on holiday Ivan has to have a secret meeting and pick up a suitcase. But what is in the suitcase? And will the secret police find out?

Ivan and the Daring Escape:
Ivan's friend Pyotr has been taken, by force, from his parents and is being held prisoner in a children's home. How will Ivan help his friend to get back home? And what about Pyotr's father, the pastor who has been put in gaol under false charges? Read this book and find out how Ivan outwits the secret police once again!

Ivan and the Moscow Circus
Ivan Nazaroff and his sister Katya meet Volodia, a trapeze artist with the Moscow Circus. Volodia's uncle has been imprisoned for criticizing the communist government. Can anything be done to help him? Read this book and find out how Ivan and Katya win the day once again!

Ivan and the American Journey
Ivan has surprised everyone, including himself. He has won the history prize and a trip to America with other students from across Moscow. But what will Ivan do when he discovers that there is someone in their group who wants to defect to the west? Should he help them? Is that right? Find out what Ivan decides by reading this book.

Children's Stories

 by J C Ryle

John Charles Ryle was born at Macclesfield in the north of England in 1816. The son of a wealthy banker, he was educated at Eton and Oxford University and was destined for a career in politics. Ryle was also a fine athlete who rowed and played cricket for Oxford.

As a result of hearing Ephesians chapter 2 read at church, Ryle became a Christian at the age of twenty-two and was ordained four years later, in 1842. He then ministered in several country churches before being appointed as the first Bishop of Liverpool in 1880.

Ryle was a well-known writer of many tracts and books as well as a faithful pastor. Children loved and looked up to him. This book is a compilation of the stories he read to the children in his congregation.

ISBN: 1-85792-639-0

Rainforest Adventures

by Horace Banner

The Amazon Rainforest is the oldest and largest rain forest in the world. Covering a huge area of South America it has the most varied plant and animal habitat on the planet. Read this book and you will join an expedition into the heart of the rain forest.

Discover the Tree Frog's nest, the Chamelon who can change it's colour and the very hungry Piranha fish. Even the Possum can teach a lesson about speaking out for Jesus Christ and the Parasol Ant can show us how to keep going and not give up. Then there's the brightly coloured Toucan whose call reminds us that with God we can do anything. Discover what its like to actually live in the Rain forest. Join in the adventures and experience the exciting and dangerous life of a pioneer missionary in South America.

ISBN: 1-85792-627-7

A young persons guide to knowing God

By Patricia St. John

Why did Sheikh Ali run and what did make the wall fall down? If you want to find out read Patricia St. John's collection of excellent short stories, which not only enthrall their readers but inform them about important Christian teaching at the same time.

This is an excellent book for young people which explains the theology behind the Apostle's creed. Why do we believe in God, did Jesus really conquer death? Patricia St. John's beautiful style and strong spiritual and scriptural insight explain the basic doctrines of the Christian faith with stories that stay in your mind for weeks afterwards. Backed up by prayers, thinking spots and scripture these are excellent devotions for youngsters, or brilliant tools for those organising assemblies or children's talks. This book is about connecting with God on a personal level. A must for every youth group and school library!

ISBN: 1-85792-558-0

Classic

Fiction

By Christoph Von Schmid

Mary grows up sheltered and secure in a beautiful cottage with a loving father. She learns lessons about humility, purity and forgiveness under her father's watchful gaze. However, it doesn't last. Even though she loves God and obeys him this does not protect her ultimately from the envy and hatred of others. Mary is given a generous gift of a new dress by her friend Amelia, the daughter of the local landowner. This incites envy from Juliette, Amelia's maid who had wanted the dress for herself. When Amelia's mother's ring goes missing Juliette decides to pass the blame onto Mary. Both Mary and her father are imprisoned for the crime and eventually exiled from their home. Mary learns to trust in God completely as difficulty follows after difficulty. Even when she doubts if she will ever clear her name she turns back to God who is a constant source of comfort to her. Who did steal the ring in the end? That is the final unexpected twist in the tale which makes this book a really good read.

ISBN 1-85792 -525-4

Classic Fiction

Christie's Old Organ

By O F Walton

Christie knows what it is like to be homeless and on the streets - that's why he is overjoyed to be given a roof over his head by Old Treffy, the Organ Grinder. But Treffy is old and sick and Christie is worried about him. All that Treffy wants is to have peace in his heart and a home of his own. That is what Christie wants too. Christie hears about how Heaven is like Home Sweet Home. Every time he plays it on Treffy's barrel organ he wonders if he and Treffy can find their way to God's special home. Find out how God uses Christie and the old Barrel organ and lots of friends along the way to bring Treffy and Christie to their own Home Sweet Home.

ISBN: 1-85792-523-8

Classic
Fiction

By O F Walton

Rosalie and her mother are tired of living a life with no home, no security and precious little hope. But Rosalie's father runs a travelling theatre company and the whole family is forced to travel from one town to the next year in year out. Rosalie's father has no objections but Rosalie's mother remembers a better life, before she was married when she had parents who loved her and a sister to play with. Through her memories Rosalie is introduced to the family she never knew she had. Rosalie and her mother are also introduced to somebody else - The Good Shepherd. They hear for the first time about the God who loves them and wants to rescue them and take them to his own home in Heaven. Rosalie rejoices to hear about a real home in Heaven that is waiting for her but will she finally find this other home that she has heard about - or is it too late? Will God help her find her family as he helped her find him? Of course he will!

ISBN 1-85792 -524-6

TRAIL BLAZERS

This is real life made as exciting as fiction! Any one of these trailblazer titles will take you into a world that you have never dreamed of. Have you ever wondered what it would it be like to be a hero or heroine? What would it be like to really stand out for your convictions? Meet William Wilberforce who fought to bring freedom to millions of slaves. Richard Wurmbrand survived imprisonment and torture. Corrie Ten Boom rescued many Jews from the Nazis by hiding them in a secret room! Amazing people with amazing stories!

This is a series worth collecting!

A Voice in the Dark: Richard Wurmbrand.
Written by Catherine Mackenzie

The Watchmaker's Daughter:
Corrie Ten Boom. Written by Jean Watson

The Freedom Fighter: William Wilberforce
Written by Derick Bingham

From Wales to Westminster:
Martin Lloyd-Jones.
Written by Christopher Catherwood

The Storyteller: C.S. Lewis
Written by Derick Bingham

An Adventure Begins: Hudson Taylor
Written by Catherine Mackenzie

The Children's Champion: George Müller
Written by Irene Howat

Servant to the Slave: Mary Slessor
Written by Catherine Mackenzie

Lights in Lisu Land: Isobel Kuhn
Written by Irene Howat

CHRISTIAN FOCUS

Good books with the real message of hope!

Christian Focus Publications publishes biblically-accurate books for adults and children.

If you are looking for quality Bible teaching for children then we have a wide and excellent range of Bible story books - from board books to teenage fiction, we have it covered.

You can also try our new Bible teaching Syllabus for 3-9 year olds and teaching materials for pre-school children.

These children's books are bright, fun and full of biblical truth, an ideal way to help children discover Jesus Christ for themselves. Our aim is to help children find out about God and get them enthusiastic about reading the Bible, now and later in their lives.

**Find us at our web page:
www.christianfocus.com**